□ □   With "Vertical and Horizontal," Lillian Ross, already well known as a reportorial writer, makes her first appearance as a writer of fiction. Miss Ross has been an innovator in casting factual reports in fictional form. Now, as might have been expected, her fiction has all the reality and palpability of fact.

Her story is about a young New York doctor named Spencer Fifield, who, in the author's words, has a head that is packed with a multitude of notions, theories, and clichés about life and love, soaked up from his friends and from his bumbling psychoanalyst, Dr. Blauberman; who, from this same analyst, receives rules, regulations, definitions, directions, admonitions, boos, and cheers, all of which he carefully memorizes; and who makes his way from a bog of intellectual hand-me-downs to full membership in what Dr. Blauberman calls "the human race."

As we follow Spencer Fifield's progress, we encounter a number of patients — including those he himself classifies as "Fifield's screwballs" and "Fifield's odd-ball-screwballs"— and a resplendent gallery of medical colleagues, plus a few

(Continued on back flap)

★

VERTICAL
AND
HORIZONTAL

★

by

LILLIAN ROSS

SIMON AND SCHUSTER
NEW YORK

1963

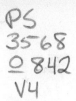

LIBRARY OF CONGRESS CATALOG CARD NUMBER: 63–12570
MANUFACTURED IN THE UNITED STATES OF AMERICA
BY THE BOOK PRESS, BRATTLEBORO, VERMONT

To William Shawn

★

VERTICAL
AND
HORIZONTAL

★ I ★

AFTER EIGHT YEARS in his own professionally interior-decorated private office on the upper East Side, Dr. Spencer
Fifield had an internal-medicine practice that consisted of a
nice proportion of businessmen and their wives, plus a rather
large assortment of what Spencer's colleagues referred to as
"Fifield's screwballs." Spencer always smiled tolerantly when
his "screwball" patients were talked about that way, and he
often held forth at length on the obligation of the doctor to
serve one and all. His patients—except for the expendable
troublemakers, who become disgruntled with every doctor
within a few months or so—paid their bills, and Spencer, economically unburdened by a wife or other dependents, lived
alone near his office, in a three-room modern, professionally

interior-decorated apartment; had a high-fidelity stereo-phonic record-playing network, with extra speakers installed in his kitchen and bathroom; drove a white convertible; took a February vacation in a sunny climate; gave his parents an annual membership in a country club on the New Jersey shore, and had built a small house for them nearby, where they spent the summer months; had an investment broker, who steered him more or less wisely; and could easily afford to pay for five twenty-five-dollar psychoanalytic hours every week.

Spencer had a fairly high turnover rate among the super-screwball patients whom he classified in his own mind as "oddball-screwballs," but there seemed to be an endless sup-ply of them, all with an abundant fund of sordid woes—sadistic husbands who beat up their wives; sadistic wives who beat up their husbands; widows requiring special erotic attentions; a strip-teaser obsessed with the temptations of suicide; a middle-aged social worker in love with one of her casework Puerto Rican schoolboys; an adolescent obesity-problem girl with a hysterical mother—to keep Spencer busy playing the role of father confessor. The businessmen pa-tients, preoccupied with money, didn't bother Spencer very much, even if they were on a first or second coronary. They talked very little, took his prescriptions, and promised to try to follow instructions. However, the businessmen's wives, for the most part, looked to Spencer, confided in him, leaned on him, along with the screwballs and the oddball-screwballs. He advised them all. He guided them. He listened to them. His strength rarely failed him, no matter how detailed the plea, or where, or when. The patients never seemed to ques-tion his competence in the role. He had the M.D., didn't he? It never occurred to Spencer to question his competence, either. They asked for it, didn't they?

10

Spencer enjoyed his medical practice. His colleagues' skepticism about the large number of screwballs he sent them for referral was outweighed by the fact that he sent them plenty of prompt-paying patients. There certainly were enough surgeons, heart specialists, G.I. men, orthopedists, gynecologists, obstetricians, radiologists, pediatricians, and hematologists who kept Spencer's name high up on their roster of capable internists. He worked morning, afternoon, and night. His patients knew they could telephone him at 4 A.M. and have him at their bedside in a matter of minutes. He was the favorite doctor of his colleagues for their sick mothers, fathers, uncles, and aunts. Spencer had a fine reputation as a diagnostician. He had a kind of sixth sense, Spencer himself liked to say, for finding the source of trouble. Every now and then, an older man at Spencer's hospital would try to give him some advice about holding down on the extent to which he might complicate a case with extraneous matters, such as becoming personally involved with the patient. But Spencer could never grasp what the older man was talking about. One elderly gynecologist, accustomed to dealing with happy pregnancies, found himself enlisted in a program, arranged by Spencer, to force an alcoholic female who was resistant to surgery into the hospital by having her niece sign the required documents. A kindly, peace-loving man, he was shocked, and tried to explain to Spencer that such drastic programs were hardly called for—that time and patience would bring the woman around to doing what was best for her health. But Spencer was adamant, and put another man on the case.

Spencer could actually find as much relaxation value, as he put it, in his practice as he could in going to the theatre or to Carnegie Hall concerts. He often spent several hours on a single house call to the home of one of his businessmen.

He liked to arrange these calls to coincide with the dinner hour. He was always confident of being welcome at the table. Wives, especially, were delighted to feed him, and the husbands appreciated the way he always took over the conversation, so that they were free to concentrate on the meal. It was usually the husband who warranted the medical call, but most of the time it was simply a matter of "Just put me back on my feet, Doctor," and a lot of them didn't leave their beds for dinner. If the wife was sick, there was usually a cook or a maid who knew the enthusiastic routine of getting a Scotch-and-soda and a good steak down the tired, hardworking doctor. Spencer played confidant to husbands and wives impartially, and he was drawn into their separate conspiracies. The strange sexual arrangements those wives adjusted themselves to! Spencer was a sympathetic audience, down to the minutiae, and he was always eager to be told more. With several of the businessmen husbands, he was also enlisted in such conspiracies as taking care of the man's secretary, her mother, four brothers, and a couple of loose children—all bills paid by the businessman.

At the age of thirty-eight, Spencer did not find his bachelorhood a handicap in his practice. When he went to his colleagues' dinner parties, he often found himself torn between sitting with the husbands and talking hospital shop and sitting with the wives and basking in his own Solomonlike status during discussions of such child-rearing subjects as bed-wetting, slow readers, hatred of fathers, hatred of teachers, psychoanalysis for children, traditional versus progressive schooling, Maine versus Montana for summer camps, and the dangers of adolescent sex. He enjoyed talking. It didn't matter too much who was listening. In his head he carried around an up-to-the-minute portfolio on all the good and liberal causes. Most of his women patients were delighted to learn that Spencer was a bachelor. He was short and stocky, with thinning light-brown hair, which he wore in a crew cut, and he had a long, mild face with even, neatly spaced out features. Much of the time, he didn't project his voice too loudly. As a matter of fact, he had a tendency to swallow his words. Once in a while, Spencer let himself go with an overeager and overindulgent woman patient, even though it was certain to wind up with her leaving him for another doctor. Generally, he avoided what he considered something of a chore anyway. But he always let it be known that he was open to meeting what he called "wife material." At times, in making a house call on a middle-aged patient, he might find a boy or girl of college age sulking in the living room. Spencer would be quick to take a hand at what called "bringing them out." If he stayed on for dinner, the boy or girl sometimes turned unfriendly, sized him up, asked him questions about medicine, or treated him with coolness or suspicion. But Spencer had a full stock of knowledgeable questions devised to bring them out, such as "How's the winter carnival?" or "The old *Spectator* still as good as it used to be?" or "I hear they're using green canvas book bags at Skidmore now" or "I'll bet you miss that handsome young president of yours at Sarah Lawrence." Simultaneously, as a kind of automatic exercise, Spencer would look them over, adding up their qualifications as wife or husband material.

Spencer's patients knew a lot about him—for the simple reason that he liked to tell them. They knew that he had lived all his life on Manhattan's upper East Side; that his father sold insurance; that he had attended the Riverdale School, Amherst, and P. & S.; that he had spent three months during his Navy years in World War II on a cruiser; that he was expert at dancing the cha-cha-cha. Most of his patients knew that he had been getting psychoanalyzed over a period of years, and that he considered it helpful in many ways to his own practice of medicine. As a matter of fact, he had sent several of his patients, as well as friends, to his own psychoanalyst, including a twenty-year-old painter from a Jewish banking family. The painter had a venereal disease contracted from another man. Spencer kept his psychoanalyst, Dr. Al Blauberman, up to date on the latest adventures of many of his screwballs, and the psychoanalyst confided in Spencer more than once that he found the oddball-screwballs most interesting of all. It was terribly tiresome, the psychoanalyst told Spencer, dealing with these dull, dull housewives, all of whom were practically alike.

A few weeks after Spencer had sent the twenty-year-old painter to Dr. Blauberman, the young man went home from an analytic session, unsuccessfully slashed his throat, and telephoned Spencer, who administered emergency treatment. Then Spencer telephoned Dr. Blauberman, who quickly said that he would come right into town, all the way from Scarsdale, even though he was right in the middle of a cookout. Forty-five minutes later, he turned up at the young man's apartment, looking scared. He was most sympathetic, helping Spencer fix the bandages on the young painter, who kept trying to tell Spencer that the psychoanalyst was inept, heavy-handed, and no psychoanalyst. But the two doctors calmed him down, and Spencer gave him a sedative. And the psychoanalyst sat with the young man well into the night, telling Spencer that the young painter's suicide attempt was just one of those things that happened; that he couldn't have foreseen or forestalled it; that one must never blame oneself for a patient's suicide; that the *best* analysts had suffered them.

14

Spencer felt strangely elated. He felt like an equal in this analytic consultation. And the analyst seemed to be feeling better, too. The incident further solidified Spencer's faith in his analyst.

Spencer got reports on these patients-in-common directly from Dr. Blauberman, when he was in his Vertical Position, before or after he lay down on the analytic couch. In his Horizontal Position, Spencer confined his talk and reports to the subject of himself, or what he hoped was himself. This Vertical-Horizontal Position stuff was a big joke, strictly between Spencer and his psychoanalyst. And, in its own way, it was always good for a laugh. A real cheerer-upper.

After a particularly tortured fifty minutes, during which Spencer went over the same rugged, agonized terrain he had been covering on the analytic couch for years—boxed-in, helpless, defeated, numb, unable to see, unable to hear, unable to feel; trying desperately to soak in through his brain-head the notions, the theories, the jargon, the clichés, and the patterns of feeling alive; and knowing that when he left his beloved analyst's office he could pretend to feel, or die to feel, or claim he felt, but he *could not feel*—the analyst would utter the mechanics of a short laugh and say, in the ambiguous accent he had developed somewhere along his own rocky road up the social scale, "So. Now we are in Vertical Position. So how did you find our young painter's flu last night? Hmmm? Is he really with fever? Too sick to come to his analyst?"

And Spencer would smile miserably and tell him. And the analyst would tell Spencer what a fine doctor Spencer was and how lucky his patients were to have him to lean on. The analyst would sometimes make Spencer feel that they were in some kind of holy cause together. Arm in arm. Together.

"So. We will make our young painter friend well. No?"
The analyst, who had been born in the Williamsburg section
of Brooklyn, had adopted a number of speech mannerisms
from Middle European big-wheel psychoanalysts, in the various stages of training he had passed through, such as, "So?,"
"No?," "So," "Hmmm?," and "Mmmm." *They* were all trying
to be Freud. Why shouldn't he?

"Someday, Dr. Fifield, we will see to it that our young
painter friend is able to have a wife, a home, and his painting. He will be able to give love. We will see to it. No? His
family will thank us for what we do here. Hmmm?"

"Yes, Dr. Blauberman," Spencer would say to his analyst,
while a small—a very, very small—part of him wanted to
scream out. "What about *me?* Will *I?* Will *I* have a wife? A
home? Will *I* have give-love?"

But Dr. Blauberman, contrary to the say-whatever-you-
please-and-anything-goes routine, had let it be known a long
time ago that he was not to be screamed at.

"So. What is the name of the bank the young man's father
is the president of? Hmmm?"

Spencer would mumble the name of the bank and leave.

Spencer occasionally took advantage of his Vertical Position to ask for advice about some of the cases he played
father confessor in. But Dr. Blauberman could be pretty
tough and rigid and uninterested in giving out advice regard-
ing cases that he felt were not worthy of his time. He told
Spencer to save *those* cases for Horizontal Position.

"This is part of your own emotional attitude toward this
woman you speak of. This friend of your cousin. Yes?
Mmmm."

So Spencer lay down on the couch and spoke of the woman
in question, the unhappy wife sent to him by one of his

16

cousins in Bridgeport. The woman had a husband in the candy business and three children in boarding school. She had peculiar stomach symptoms. Spencer had tried several new drugs on her, without results. Finally, he had sent her to one of his favorite G.I. men, a *Harvard* Med School man, a man he thought was a gentleman. It then developed that the lady was coming in from Bridgeport twice a week regularly to see the G.I. man after office hours. "Frankly, I feel responsible, Dr. Blauberman. After all, she's my cousin's friend."

"The woman is over twenty-one? So."

"Yes, Dr. Blauberman. But frankly she's—well, *stu*pid. She has a fine husband in Bridgeport. In the candy business."

"She needs analysis," Dr. Blauberman said, without pause, without doubt. "Forget it. Let him sleep with her." Dr. Blauberman sounded resentful, almost jealous. "So. *Why* do you feel responsible for this woman? Tell me. Why? Hmmm?"

Dr. Blauberman could be damn sweet, loving, and helpful to Spencer, especially when it came to problems he and Spencer had in common. For instance, it was Spencer's dream someday, if he did get married, to marry a girl who had gone to Barnard. When he was at Amherst, he had dated a Barnard girl—he had always been too shy to kiss her—and suddenly she had married one of his classmates. That had been that. Spencer thought it was a simple explanation of why he was naturally interested in Barnard girls.

"Too simple. Mmmm. We must find out *why*." Then, with an exasperated sigh, Dr. Blauberman spent the balance of thirty-two minutes in telling Spencer the long story of how he, Al Blauberman, son of a chicken plucker in Williamsburg, had needed—and had found—a Barnard girl to sustain his

17

faith in himself. He had married a Barnard girl. She was the mother of his two splendid children, both of whom were very popular in their Scarsdale school. But it hadn't been simple. You think it was simple? Hmmm? So. Oh, no. Because between chicken plucking (for Dr. Blauberman's boyhood had been spent among the feathers, under the whiplash of his vengeful chicken-plucking father) and Barnard, between Williamsburg and Scarsdale, what Dr. Blauberman had not suffered! The snubs, the slurs, the insults of boys who lived securely on Riverside Drive! Then—carried into the present time by the momentum of his own reminiscence—Dr. Blauberman confided to Spencer that he still suffered similar snubs and insults from *other psychoanalysts*. The ones who thought they were so good, just because they had worked with Freud! The ones who had come over here in the thirties, refugees! The ones who had studied in Austria, Holland, Hungary!

"Well, frankly, Dr. Blauberman, I guess I need that kind of social-bolstering values. I can't help it if—" Spencer began, trying to get back to what he was saying. But by then the hour was over.

"So," Dr. Blauberman said, still panting from his tirade about himself. "You will continue where you left off. See you tomorrow."

And Spencer got into Vertical Position and left.

Dr. Blauberman was definitely a big help to Spencer in his dealings with women. Take that long-legged blond divorcée who was a mistress of ceremonies on a television game program. She telephoned Spencer one Sunday morning just before dawn and said she was sick. He rushed right over and gave her a shot of penicillin. Then she offered Spencer a drink and asked him if he wanted to stick around and read

18

the funny papers. "Daniel won't mind," she had said. Daniel was her nine-year-old son, asleep in the next room.

"I hung around and had breakfast there," Spencer told Dr. Blauberman the next day. "And, frankly, I think I felt something."

"You think you can become emotionally involved with this woman? Mmmm. You think?"

Spencer thought.

In the middle of his thinking, the analyst said, "Not so much thinking. *Don't* think."

Puzzled, Spencer tried to stop thinking.

"So. Think it over," Dr. Blauberman then said. "You should *have* involvement with a woman, with this, this—hmmm?"

"Clarissa."

"With Clarissa. So."

So. Spencer did. Clarissa was amenable, although Spencer often came across another man hanging around. Morris. He was in television, too, and Daniel was crazy about Morris, and was always roughhousing with him. Anyway, Spencer reported to Dr. Blauberman that he was involved—had a relationship—with Clarissa. Two months later, he made a house call on a patient referred to him—in the usual exchange program in medicine—by the wayward G.I. man. She was a soft, plump graduate of Barnard, class of '57, who had left her family to live alone in the Village and write a novel. She brought out a strange, protective sensation in Spencer's breast.

Dr. Blauberman advised breaking off with Clarissa and starting in with Barnard.

"Frankly, I don't know how to do it," Spencer said, from the couch. "What'll I say to Clarissa?"

"Just tell her it's finished. You don't want recriminations, tell her. Mmmm. No arguments. No recriminations. Stand firm."

Spencer went to Clarissa and told her it was all over.

"Of course, honey," Clarissa said, absent-mindedly. "It's O.K. I understand all about your troubles and all. Don't worry about a thing."

"I don't want any recriminations," Spencer said, standing firm.

"Of course, honey. There isn't anything to worry about, don't you understand? Take it easy. Everything is hunky-dory."

"No recriminations," Spencer said stubbornly. "No arguments. I just wanted to tell you myself."

"What, honey?"

"No recriminations."

Clarissa giggled. "Who's recriminating, honey? Take it easy."

At that point, Morris arrived, leading Daniel on stilts.

The next day, Spencer reported proudly to his analyst that he had stood firm.

The future novelist was a dud, too. Every time he had a date with her, she found a way of making it a crowd. With her two roommates. Three silly, irritating girls. They listened with impatience to Spencer's stories of Riverdale, Amherst, and the Navy, and then they left him out and talked to each other—in code, most of the time, and with a lot of shrill laughter. Spencer found himself paying dinner checks for four. Not that he couldn't afford it. It was the principle of the thing.

Then another Barnard girl came into his life. Class of '53. Real wife material, he told Dr. Blauberman, pleading. Her name was Annie Melvin. She was working in one of the labs at the hospital. Her brother was a doctor. She was dark-haired, pretty. Sort of pretty. He was almost sure she was pretty. She didn't talk much. She didn't wear much makeup. She didn't have a mustache. The future novelist *and* her two roommates all had a mustache. He hated girls with a mustache. He had taken Annie to dinner the night before, and after dinner they had gone to the Five Spot. She loved jazz. She dressed a little on the beatnik side. And not décolleté. In talking to Dr. Blauberman, he strained to recall the pat diagrams he had accumulated in his head over the years with the analyst. Maybe she was afraid-of-herself-as-an-adult-woman. Maybe she didn't-know-how-to-give. Maybe she hadn't-developed-mature-values. He had asked her if she had ever been analyzed, and she had laughed and said that most analysts were squares. It was hard to tell what she was. Whether she had give-love. But she had gone to Barnard. Real wife material. He had told her all about Riverdale and Amherst and the Navy. Most of his important war stories. The three months on the cruiser. All the sailors to whom he was father confessor. He was quite sure she was pretty. No, Annie did nothing to encourage him. Not really. No, she wouldn't go home with him when he asked her. But she was apologetic about turning him down. She really seemed sorry. Maybe she was just scared-of-men. She always spoke softly to him. She seemed to like him. She listened to him. She sounded sad.

"Hmmm?" Dr. Blauberman said.

"I'm almost positive she's pretty," Spencer said.

One cold November morning, Spencer came to Dr. Blauberman in a terrible state of excitement, and, not waiting to go from Vertical to Horizontal, said that Annie was in the

21

hospital. She was going to have an emergency appendectomy. "Luckily, I heard about it in time," Spencer said, finally taking to the couch. "I'm going up to the O.R. from here and watch." Then he couldn't think of another blessed thing that hour to say to his analyst.

The operation went beautifully, and Spencer was on hand in Annie's room the moment she woke up. He was smoking a cigarette nervously, in quick, short puffs. The nurse on duty in the room asked him to put out the cigarette. He jubilantly threw it to the floor and put his heel on it. Spencer was the first person Annie saw. She smiled.

"Hi, they did a beautiful job on you," he told her. "Beautiful cutting."

Annie wet her lips. "You saw it?"

"I was right there."

"Why? Who asked you to be there?" She had stopped smiling.

He didn't understand. Annie closed her eyes. The nurse told Spencer that Annie should be left alone to rest and sleep. But Spencer had something important to tell her. "My analyst was making sympathetic, clucking noises about you," he said.

Annie opened her eyes. "Did it bother you to watch me being sliced open?"

"Routine." Spencer sniffed. "I wish you could have heard those little clucks of sympathy from Dr. Blauberman. He sends you his best regards."

Three days later, Annie was walking around, feeling chipper. But she left the "No Visitors" sign on the door. The sign didn't keep Spencer out. He barged right in, without knocking, usually when she was having a meal. He was beginning to have a proprietary interest in Annie, and he was beginning to feel even more protective toward her than he ever had toward Barnard '57, he had told Dr. Blauberman.

22

"So. How's our patient?" Spencer walked in breezily on Annie just as she was starting her lunch.

Annie put down a lamb chop and lay back on her pillow. Spencer lit a cigarette. Annie gave a few choking-cough hints, which went unnoticed by an enthusiastic Spencer.

"So. Mmmm," he said. "I told my analyst about your 'No Visitors' sign. Frankly, at first I was disturbed. I thought you were wrong. Anti-social. Hmmm? But my analyst says you're right. He says you want to rest."

"You've got some analyst, man," Annie said, her eyes closed.

Spencer was delighted. "He's a wonderful person, Dr. Blauberman."

When Annie got out of the hospital, she took a couple of weeks off in Jamaica. So she wasn't around when Spencer got George Sunshine, the movie star, as a patient. A medical-school classmate now practicing in Hollywood had sent George Sunshine to Spencer. It was Spencer's first real, famous, big-time movie actor. At the first visit, in the office, Spencer was so nervous during the workup that his throat kept catching, and he gave tense little sniffs. His hands shook during the examination.

"Don't pay any attention to the George Sunshine," said George Sunshine. "My studio thought it was a new gimmick when they handed it to me. Real wild. They were fed up with all the Tabs and Bats and Rods and Bucks. Now they don't want *me*, but I'm stuck with the name. My real name is Stanford Fleming, which I personally think is O.K."

The movie star was pretty nervous himself. His hands shook, too. He had cracked up four automobiles in the past year. His eyes sparkled with the cellophane-covered look, with the special quality that goes with tranquillizers, barbiturates, and other sedatives. He smelled of whiskey. He wore an impeccably tailored oxford-gray suit. He was thin, angular, possibly tubercular, and utterly without hope.

"You going to do a play?" Spencer asked him. "That why you're here?"

"I'm here because I've got nowhere else to be but here," said George Sunshine.

"That's the thing now—to do a play," said Spencer, who didn't always catch what was being said to him.

"Just call me Jack Lemmon," said George Sunshine.

"Lemmon's got it made," Spencer said. "He's a marvellous actor. He's so funny."

"You bet, Doc." George Sunshine gave a weak smile. "I'm one of his most passionate fans."

George Sunshine sounded peculiar. But, after all, he might be another screwball. "I guess Lemmon proves that Hollywood doesn't kill all talent," Spencer said chummily. "For people like you and Lemmon, they can do anything to you out there, but they can't touch you where you *live*."

"Sure, Doc. I've got to hand it to you, the way you've got it all figured out." George Sunshine put a friendly arm around Spencer. "Now, how about some of those little red pills?"

He asked for twice the usual potency and four times the usual quantity of Seconal. Spencer gave him the prescription.

From then on, George Sunshine was a steady topic on the agenda with Dr. Blauberman. Wife material as a whole would have to wait. The movie actor, Dr. Blauberman said, sounded very interesting—certainly more interesting than housewives.

Spencer didn't hear from George Sunshine for three weeks after that first visit, even though he had told the actor to have a checkup once a week. In the meantime, he spent all his psychoanalytic time talking about the actor. Dr. Blauberman learned that George Sunshine had been married to a beautiful model, who had left him after one year for a Brazilian mining tycoon.

"These actors lead very unreal lives, frankly," said Spencer. "All they care about is exhibiting themselves."

"And did the actor get his divorce in California?" Dr. Blauberman asked.

"Apparently."

"So. Community division of property. So."

"They don't relate well to reality," Spencer said.

A few days before Christmas, Spencer made a house call, at dinnertime, on Hiram (High Fidelity) Stone, the electronics king, who tried every now and then to buy Spencer all for himself. The furthest he had got along these selfish lines was Spencer's exclusive attentions on a three-week trip to Europe, financed by Mr. Stone. Spencer's stereophonic high-fidelity system had been obtained courtesy of the king, as a small token of appreciation. The electronics king had had intermittent rashes of a violent sort, which required ordinary attentions. But Mr. Stone didn't want anyone but Spencer to know about his odd symptoms. So, every week, Spencer went up to attend Mr. Stone in his Fifth Avenue coöperative penthouse, where Mr. Stone shared the fullness of his life and laughter with Mrs. Stone, a washed-out, good-hearted blonde with the permanently yellowish complexion of too many winters under tropical skies. She rarely appeared without a bracelet of golden chains on her wrist, in quadruplicate, from which hung golden charms roughly the size of crab apples. She even wore it when she was sick in bed. The Stones had a valet and a cook, a married couple of middle age, who had once worked for Darryl Zanuck in Beverly Hills.

Spencer fixed Mr. Stone up, and, his arm linked with Mrs. Stone's jangling arm, was led to a table, where a monumental slice of roast beef awaited him. He took a bite, then jumped up, saying he had to telephone in for messages. It always made an effective impression to call in for messages in front of patients.

There was a message to call George Sunshine as soon as possible.

Spencer couldn't contain himself. He left the rest of his roast beef. He left the Stones and went out into the night. It was snowing. He couldn't get his car started. Anxiously he grabbed his black bag from the car and ran for a skidding taxi. He missed it. He slipped on the icy sidewalk and skinned the hand holding the bag. He had left his gloves in the car. It took him twenty minutes to get a taxi and almost as long to go fourteen blocks to the East Sixties near the river, where George Sunshine had sublet a town house. When he rang the doorbell, he noticed that his skinned hand was bleeding. He quickly wiped it off on a handkerchief inside his pocket.

The door was opened by a young man with a tiny, pouting mouth, large nostrils, and whitish-blond hair falling over his forehead, who had on a white shirt open at the collar, white pants, white socks, and white sneakers. He stared at Spencer without asking him in.

"I'm Dr. Fifield," Spencer said.

"Ooh, my God!" the young man said, and led Spencer inside, where he watched as Spencer took off his coat and then once more wiped his skinned hand against the handkerchief in his pocket.

"Georgie is crocked," the young man said in a nonchalant, nasalized drawl. "I put in the call for you myself. I found your name on the bottle."

26

"Quick thinking," Spencer said, and tried to give the young man a smile. Through a partly open door, Spencer could see a warm-looking living room with a grand piano, a number of green plants, and a fluffy white rug. A record was playing loudly. It was Pearl Bailey singing "Too Tired":

Tired of the tears I shed
Tired of living in the red . . .

"Pearly-Mae," Spencer said knowingly to the young man in white. He followed this remark with another smile, and then a tense cough. "I love these old town houses," he said, looking around. "They remind me of the house I grew up in. My grandfather's house. I've always wanted to get a house like this myself."

"Yeah. Georgie is upstairs. Don't you want to see him? First bedroom on your right."

Spencer started up the stairs, and although the young man had seemed to be sending him up alone, he came up behind him. The bedroom had a bright-green rug. A purple bedspread on a Hollywood-size bed, with bright-green throw pillows. Drapes matching the purple bedspread. Three ebony chests in a row stood facing the bed. A full-grown boxer was stretched across the foot of the bed, his head up, his tongue out, his eyes dripping rheumily. And on the bright-green throw pillows lay George Sunshine, fully clothed in his oxford-gray, with a black knit tie and a white button-down-collar shirt, black silk socks, and highly polished black loafers. Without a word, the young man in white lifted himself to a sitting position on top of an ebony chest, crossed his legs, and, lighting a cigarette, inhaled deeply and blew out a stream of smoke toward the bed.

Spencer didn't have a chance to open his bag. As soon as

27

he approached the bed, George Sunshine opened his eyes and sat up, apparently cold sober. The young man in white gave a shriek of laughter, showing two even rows of newly capped teeth. "Georgie-Porgie, well, just look at you!" he said. "Bright as day. I thought I ought to call the Doctor, Georgie, when I couldn't wake you up. Because the *people* are coming."

George Sunshine yawned and, reaching over to the boxer, patted his head and smiled at Spencer, who asked him how he felt.

"As Tommy says, bright as day," George Sunshine said. "Bright as a new penny. Bright as hell."

Tommy gave another laugh and recrossed his legs. "You're a riot," he said. "Half an hour ago, I couldn't wake you up."

"Well, the Doc is here, so let's offer him a drink," George Sunshine said. He got up and, from a chest drawer, took out a bottle of Scotch and three jigger glasses. He filled them and handed one to Spencer.

"If the Doctor had telephoned before coming over, he might have saved himself a trip," Tommy said. "The message I left asked him to *tele*phone. No, thanks, I want to stay sober for the people," he said, refusing the jigger of whiskey which was being held out to him. "Give it to Beauty," he drawled, and gave a titter. The boxer on the bed, hearing his name, shook his head, dripping saliva on the purple bedspread.

George Sunshine winked at Spencer and drank the whiskey in a gulp.

"Merry Christmas!" Spencer said, in a choked voice. He wished he didn't find it so difficult to talk. Imitating the actor, he drank his whiskey in a gulp.

"*L'chaim!*" George Sunshine said, and refilled Spencer's glass. "I forgot to tell you, Doc, I became a goddam linguist

28

out in Hollywood," He took the third jigger over to Beauty, held the dog's jaws open, and forced some drink into the boxer's mouth. Tommy shrieked with laughter and, skipping over to the bed, put his cigarette in a corner of the dog's mouth. The boxer spat out both cigarette and whiskey and then sneezed.

"Oh, you Beauty! We're teaching you some bad habits!" Tommy said.

Spencer watched them uncomfortably. He took a sip of his second drink and cleared his throat. "Boxers are one of my favorite dogs," he said. "I never had a boxer myself. Frankly, all I ever had were mongrels." He was aware of being regarded with coolness by Tommy, but he didn't give it much importance. Here was a real oddball-screwball.

Tommy lit another cigarette. Two streams of smoke were exhaled heavily from the large nostrils. "Do me one big favor, Georgie. Just don't pass out again until the people have come and *gone*," he said.

George Sunshine shrugged. "Stick around, Doc," he said to Spencer. "We've got a brilliant young playwright who can't be touched where he *lives* coming over to read us his play. The play has a big juicy part in the lead."

Spencer felt proud. "I told you you ought to do a play," he said.

"The part is for Tommy," said George Sunshine. "I am bait for our little Tommy here."

"You getting Gadge to direct it?" Spencer asked in his best in-the-know manner.

Tommy gave a thin, mean scream of protest. "I don't know about *Gadge*," he said. "I may not want *Gadge*. He voted against me for the Actors' Studio. I may just settle on old Josh."

29

George Sunshine laughed. Spencer felt he ought to give a laugh, too, and he did. George Sunshine put an arm around Spencer. He was still laughing. "Stick around for the fun, Doc," he said. "The playwright is bringing Betty Bloop over. Or maybe it's Betty Boop. Or Betty Grable. No, I'm sure it's Betty Bloop, unless it's Betty Comden or somebody like that. We do a lot of socializing this time of the year."

Spencer felt light in the head. He could hear himself telling Dr. Blauberman all about it. He smiled at Tommy. "Where you going New Year's Eve?" he asked him. "To the Strasbergs' party or to the Hirschfelds' party?" Someone had once told Spencer these were the two big festive blowouts in theatrical-celebrity circles to see the New Year in.

Instead of answering him, Tommy mimicked the question in a singsong baby voice. "You going to the Strasbergs' party or you going to the Hirschfelds' party? Huh?"

Spencer could not believe his ears. He thought Tommy was making a screwball joke of some kind. Spencer took a large sip of his drink and smiled.

"For Christ's sake, Georgie, get this creep out of here," Tommy said, in harsh, nasal tones. "Before the *peo*ple get here."

Spencer still thought it was some kind of oblique way of kidding. He finished his drink, and again he smiled.

George Sunshine gave a deep sigh. "Tommy, Tommy, behave yourself," he said. He put his arm around Spencer again and walked him down the stairs. "Don't mind Tommy, Doc. Sorry you can't stay."

Out on the street, Spencer shivered. There was a terrible ringing in his ears. It was snowing harder now, and the wet flakes fell on his hair and, melting, ran down his face and the back of his neck. He turned up his overcoat collar and started

30

walking, in a daze, west. That goddam homosexual. Everything had been going so smoothly with the actor. It had promised to be such a full evening. And it was probably Tommy who was keeping the actor from returning to him as a doctor. The incident plagued him. He felt his skinned hand smarting, and then it began, really painfully, to throb. In time with the throbbing in his head. There was something more that had happened. There must have been something more. He searched for it in his mind. Suddenly, without thinking, he found himself crying. Sobbing. Deep, shaking sobs. Child crying. Little-boy crying. He could hear his own crying as though it were coming from outside himself. He was helpless to control it. He felt. He felt. But he didn't know what.

Shaking all over, he went into the nearest drugstore and telephoned Dr. Blauberman at home. It was an emergency. Dr. Blauberman would understand. It was the first time he had disturbed his analyst at home since the early months in analysis, more than ten years ago, when he couldn't stand *not* telephoning, *not* hearing the voice. He was desperate now to hear the voice, that friendly voice.

A woman's voice answered, sounding resentful, ill-tempered. "Just a minute, I'll call him." Spencer could barely keep standing in the telephone booth during that long, long minute. His knees buckled, straightened, buckled, straightened.

"Yes, Dr. Fifield. So?" The voice reached into Spencer and gave him strength. He talked fast to his analyst, tearing out the story of what had just happened to him. There had to be something Dr. Blauberman could tell him. Please, Dr. Blauberman. Dear Dr. Blauberman.

And the angel Blauberman spoke to Spencer. He somewhat

appropriated Spencer's own excitable tones, but he nevertheless spoke to Spencer. Dr. Blauberman would grant a special appointment, an *extra* fifty minutes, the very first thing in the morning, at ten minutes before eight. Wonderful Dr. Blauberman. Wonderful, good friend.

Spencer left the telephone booth, now half sobbing, half laughing. He had to keep walking. He walked the snowy streets until after midnight, searching for what he felt. He became calmer, although his head still throbbed and the black bag he carried tore at his wounded hand. He found himself wondering if Annie was back from Jamaica. He thought about calling her up. No. Not really. Wait. Wait for Dr. Blauberman.

He went home to his decorated apartment. His shoes were wet through with snow. He went into the bathroom. He turned on the light switch, which automatically threw on the stereo hi-fi. Berlioz' "Requiem" stormed into the bathroom as Spencer put antiseptic on his sore, inflamed hand. He took a hot shower. Later, he warmed some milk in a saucepan. With the warm milk, he took two half-grains of phenobarbital. He went to the living room and turned on "The Late Late Show." Wallace Beery, playing a policeman, found a crying baby in a paper box behind a garbage can. Spencer turned off the television. The crying of the baby lingered in his head. He went into the bedroom and lay down. But sleep wouldn't come. He felt the tightness in his diaphragm. Cement. Again he thought of telephoning Annie. Wait. Wait for Dr. Blauberman.

He was out of bed at six. It was still snowing outside. He drank half a quart container of orange juice. He made two fried eggs with bacon and toast and drank two cups of instant coffee. He needed a good breakfast today—something to counteract the unslept-off sedation. He didn't bother to pick up his car. He took a taxi. At seven-thirty, he was sitting in Dr. Blauberman's waiting room. Fifteen minutes later, Dr. Blauberman arrived, wearing a fur-collared storm coat against the wintry morning.

Spencer quickly headed for the couch. Dr. Blauberman stopped him. "We are Vertical this morning. No?" Dr. Blauberman's face was ruddy, expectant, aglow with the snowy new day. "So. You want to discuss our Hollywood actor. Mmmm."

"Well, yes—that is, frankly, he's got this homosexual hanging around him, draining him. . . ." His voice petered out. He remained standing, in Vertical Position, suddenly unable to remember what he wanted to say. He rubbed his eye with his knuckles. He wasn't sure what he was talking about, or what he was thinking. His head still throbbed. His hand felt stiff and sore. What was it he had felt?

"Mmmm. Our actor friend needs help. Tell me about him. He should go into analysis. He should see a good analyst? Yes?"

"Yes, Dr. Blauberman," Spencer said. "Yes."

33

I T WAS NINE-FIFTEEN at the hospital, on a Sunday night in the middle of winter, and Spencer sat in one of the private rooms puffing energetically on a cigarette and talking with enthusiasm to the twenty-year-old college girl lying flat on the white bed before him. She wasn't a regular patient. Her regular doctor, Harvey Davis, was out of town. Davis was one of the powers in the hospital; he had married into the Bernheimer family, which had three members on the hospital board. Phil Brody, who covered for Davis, was in bed with the flu, and Spencer was covering for Brody, who was so jittery about muffing something to do with a Harvey Davis patient that he had called Spencer three times from his sickbed to ask whether everything was absolutely under control.

If it wasn't, he said, he would get right over to the hospital *with* his temperature of a hundred and one. Spencer had never had a Harvey Davis patient before. This one, Susan Auerbach, was a good example of the kind of well-to-do practice, among people pretty damn high on the social and economic scale, that Davis—and Brody, for that matter—enjoyed. The Auerbach family owned valuable real estate in the city, and had owned it for a long time, too. Spencer was pleased at having Susan Auerbach *and* her family, and he was pleased at having made the correct diagnosis when he saw the girl, for the first time, that afternoon at her home. The Auerbachs lived in a duplex in one of the older apartment houses on the upper East Side; their apartment was elegant, comfortable, not ostentatious, and it had a real Dufy above a real fireplace in the living room. Spencer had hung around there for over an hour, just talking, even though it had taken him no more than ten minutes to make his diagnosis, in the girl's bright, cozy room. Harvey Davis would have no complaints about the diagnosis. Brody certainly had none when Spencer telephoned him and told him what he had found, and that he would be a damn fool to get out of bed and come over. Brody sounded relieved, actually, to stay in his bed when Spencer told him what he thought Susan had. Spencer usually guessed right about those hidden, lousy things. And in this instance he had since been proved right—both by Dr. Solender, the brain surgeon he had (with Brody's approval) brought in on the case, and by the X-ray films and other tests. Susan was admitted to the hospital for surgery. Spencer's name, along with Dr. Solender's, was up on the card outside on the girl's door. All of this on a dreary, snow-threatened Sunday when Spencer had not expected anything new or interesting to happen.

35

The girl raised her head from the pillow and tried groggily to look at him. He got up and went over to the foot of the bed. He placed his hand, in the classic medical show of reassurance, on her ankle, and let out a little laugh of pleasure. It was more than just having been proved right in his diagnosis; it was finding someone he could talk to and, in a way, get close to, as often happened with his patients. Also, it usually gave him a lift to call on a new patient, even if it was one he was taking over temporarily for another doctor. Even if the Auerbach girl had turned out to be merely a Phil Brody patient instead of a Harvey Davis one, it would have been all right. Brody had a good, solid practice—either upper-middle-class or better, and very much like Brody himself, who was about twenty years older than Spencer and had a son at Harvard Medical School. And Brody kept his patients. Some of them, Spencer knew for a fact, had stayed with Brody since he started to practice. Brody, like Harvey Davis, refused to have anything to do with screwballs, who were too demanding, too neurotic. Every now and then, Spencer would become dissatisfied with his screwball patients, and would resolve to build his own practice along Davis-Brody-type lines. What's more, he would resolve to get married and have children, and to build his life along Davis-Brody lines, too. Spencer had once come close to having a date with a niece of the Bernheimers, on one of her weekends in from school, but she had missed her train or something and the date had never come off. That was over three years ago. Spencer still talked about it a lot.

Susan's room looked out on the park. Outside, there was a damp frost in the air. Spencer said that if *he* ran the hospital he would put Dufy prints on the walls instead of the kind of pastoral calendar art they had now. Susan raised her head,

trying to look at the picture on the wall facing her bed—
white-and-brown cows in a field of green, green grass. She
didn't make it. She put her head down. Steam hissed from
the radiator, keeping the edges of the windows trimmed
unevenly with mist but leaving a ragged oval in the center
clear to a view of the lamplit park. All kinds of poignant
noises floated sharply up from the street and from the park:
a man on the street called to someone; a dog barked; an automobile horn was pushed five times; a policeman's horse gal-
loped on the pavement. If Susan's vision had not been im-
paired by her condition, she might have seen, from her lying-
down position, the tops of the taller trees in the park, with
spotty patches of snow clinging to the high branches. Spencer
didn't bother to look out. He was completely caught up in
the presence of this girl in the room. He was in no hurry to
leave. There was no rush. They hadn't even done the spinal
tap on the girl yet. Spencer felt unusually relaxed. Very
often, when he felt particularly lonely and cut off from the
regular routines of life followed by his married colleagues,
he would drop in on his patients in the hospital during the
supper hour, gossip with them, find out about their jobs or
their love troubles or family troubles or money troubles, and
give them advice. Sometimes he would spend a quiet half
hour or so in patients' rooms reading their gift books. With
the intellectuals, he could talk about literature and other
cultural subjects. When he ran into patients' visitors, he
would stay and pass the gift cookies to them, talking like an
old friend. When his patients didn't feel quite up to food, he
would eat their hospital-tray suppers. If they did feel up to
it, he would nibble at their leftovers. He had found that almost all his patients—especially in the hospital—when
they felt frightened or in pain, liked to have their doctor

hanging around. His presence added a measure of reassurance, of protection. He was wanted in a way that gave a special sort of meaning to his own life. When he walked into a patient's room, he was looked at with automatic respect. Automatic dependence. Automatic love.

The girl on the bed now looked at him with automatic respect and dependence and love. Spencer had a feeling of closeness to this girl. It wasn't an idea. It was a feeling. He was almost sure it felt like a feeling. The morning before, Dr. Blauberman had been telling him he intellectualized too much. About everything. Including everything he did.

"Frankly, Dr. Blauberman, I think I don't intellectualize as much as I used to," Spencer said, from the couch.

"Mmmm," Dr. Blauberman said. "You intellectualize when you should feel. No?"

"I don't know how to shut it off, frankly. Thinking. How can I make myself feel?"

"Hmmm. Mmmm?" Dr. Blauberman said. "So. You will know when it happens. Mmmm?"

Just outside the door, in the dimly lighted corridor, which had been cleared of all other visitors, Mr. and Mrs. Auerbach and their eighteen-year-old son Paul were waiting—shattered, dazed, helpless, in blank terror—for Dr. Spencer Fifield to emerge and give them some further word on the course of action to be followed. Not that there would be any change in plan. Dr. Fifield had made that clear, and Dr. Solender, the brain surgeon, had briskly confirmed the facts. It wasn't so bad, Dr. Fifield had told them lightly. It could be worse. They had the facts. Accept them. And he had taken off to arrange for further tests. With the facts tearing at their hearts, they had sat quietly in Susan's room, shaking, trying

38

to look steady, trying to smile, trying to talk to the girl in the bed. Then Dr. Fifield had returned to the room, smoking breezily, looking dimpled, seeming much younger than his age, and enjoying himself mightily in this fearful moment over which he had supreme control. Looking with expectation at Susan, he had asked Mr. and Mrs. Auerbach and Paul to wait outside. So they had gone out to the corridor. There they stood close together—handsome, smartly dressed, well-mannered, but unaccustomed to sudden tragedy, unequipped for horror.

Private nurses attending other rooms scuttled back and forth in the corridor, their eyes averted from the Auerbachs, their attention on the particular patient of their eight-hour attachment. The Auerbachs pressed themselves up against the wall, embarrassed that they might be in the way. Postoperative patients came out of their rooms for their nightly walks, and the Auerbachs seemed further embarrassed by their direct, curious stares as the patients shuffled awkwardly past them. The head floor nurse approached. "Would you wait in the waiting room around the corner?" she said, impatient, unsmiling. She had an overly pale face, bright dabs of rouge on her cheeks, graying hair flattened by the nurse's cap, and steel-rimmed spectacles. Her uniform was wrinkled and not impeccably white. She had a heavy cold. Sunday night was her Monday morning, and she was in no mood for irregularities.

"Thank you, but we'd like to wait right here, if you don't mind," Mr. Auerbach said. "Dr. Fifield asked us to step out here for a moment. He's in there with our daughter." His wife and son nodded agreement with this incontrovertible statement and looked pleadingly, in silence, at the nurse.

"You've been standing out here twenty minutes against the

39

rules. We've got our rules, you know. . . . All right. If that's what you want," she added, and quickly moved away from them. If she stood there, they'd be trying to hand *her* their fear. No, thanks.

She went into the room on the left at the end of the corridor. The door to the room was open, and she left it open. A television set inside the room was turned on full blast. It emitted sounds of Rochester engaged in hoarse conversational battle over penury with his boss, Jack Benny, and of metallic TV-audience laughs, like weird cacophonies from another planet.

Mr. Auerbach turned to his wife. "O.K., Mil?" he asked.

She nodded, her lips tightly compressed, working off the last remaining flecks of the lipstick applied so very long ago. A black alligator purse hung from one arm, and she wore black alligator pumps. One hand clutched the back of the other, and she held them both pressed against her waist.

"Mom, maybe you ought to sit down." Paul Auerbach said, in a reedy voice. He was skinny and tall, with a small, round face resting on a shirt collar that had round tabs held together with a straight gold pin. He stood a couple of inches taller than his father, who wore the same kind of collar and pin.

Jack Benny's nasalized complaints to Don Wilson came at them from the room at the end of the corridor. Mr. Auerbach gave his wife a small smile. "If you want to sit down, Mil, we'll call you as soon as Dr. Fifield comes out."

"What's he *doing* in there?" Mrs. Auerbach asked. She had a low, pleasant voice, marred slightly by the sound of her pain. "He said for a *moment*. . . . I don't want to sit down, Ernie. Do you?"

"I'm fine, Mil. I'm sure he'll be out soon."

40

"What a time for Dr. Davis to be away!" Mrs. Auerbach said. "My God, what a time! At least he's known her since she was a baby."

"Harvey Davis is one of these two-vacations-a-year doctors, summer and winter," Mr. Auerbach said.

"Way down in God knows where in the West Indies!" Mrs. Auerbach said.

"I don't mean he doesn't need it," Mr. Auerbach said. "He had that coronary two years ago."

"We really need him, Ernie. We need somebody we *know*."

"This fellow"—Mr. Auerbach inclined his head in the direction of Susan's room—"seems to be good. A bit young, but he seems to know what it's all about. We're just used to Harvey Davis."

"Do you want to eat something, Ernie?" Mrs. Auerbach asked, as though the question were a sequitur. "You must be starved. All you had was breakfast."

Mr. Auerbach shook his head. "But you ought to have something," he said. "You were up all night with her. You didn't even have breakfast."

"So were you," Mrs. Auerbach said.

"How about a cup of tea? Paul could run out to a drugstore or someplace."

"I don't want a cup of tea," Mrs. Auerbach said, almost irritably. "I don't want anything."

"There's a hamburger place right near here," Paul Auerbach said. "I got a very good hamburger there before. They have tea. I could bring you a hamburger, Mom, too." He blushed and looked uneasy.

"I can't eat," Mrs. Auerbach said.

"I can't, either," Mr. Auerbach said. He glanced anxiously at Susan's door. "Harvey's answering service couldn't locate either of the two doctors he left to cover for him," he said. "You know that nice Dr. Brody we had that time for your grippe? I tried to get him again. Harvey always has him cover for him, but Brody's service said that Dr. Fifield was covering for *him*. I'm sure Dr. Brody wouldn't have anybody covering for him who wasn't *good*."

"Dad?" Paul said. "Maybe we could telephone Dr. Davis long distance and talk to him. Ask him if he thinks Dr. Fifield is a good man for this."

"I tried that before you came home. He's on some damn little island down there, cut off from everything. The whole idea, I guess, is to get away from the ringing telephone."

"What a time for him to be away!" Mrs. Auerbach said. She stared at the door to Susan's room. "What's he *doing* in there?"

"Take it easy, Mil," Mr. Auerbach said.

"Dr. Fifield must be a good man, Mom." Paul said. "After all, he's on the staff of the hospital. You don't get on the staff if you don't measure up. And didn't you think he was sort of trying to be nice? In the house, I mean?"

"Susie seemed to like him," Mr. Auerbach said.

"Poor sweet baby, she—" Mrs. Auerbach stopped and brought herself under control. She switched hands, bottom to top, top to bottom, holding each other. She said, with bitterness, "If she's got what they say she's got, her mind isn't exactly clear to decide what she likes or doesn't like."

The three Auerbachs avoided looking at each other. Finally, Mr. Auerbach said, "Both Dr. Fifield and Dr. Solender say we must remember these things are often localized and not malignant and easily removed. But they have to go ahead with the operation. Then they say she'll be perfectly O.K., if everything goes all right. They both feel sure."

"Susie will be O.K., Mom. Everybody says so."

"Then what's keeping him in there? Don't you think we can just go in?" Mrs. Auerbach asked.

"We have to observe their routine," Mr. Auerbach said. "It's that way in everything. This is no exception."

"I keep thinking it's one of those horrible nightmares you wake up from and everything is all right. But I guess that's what everybody thinks," she added. "It's so unfair. So unfair. All those dances she went to Christmas week. She was never so happy. She never looked so lovely. Her junior year has been her best."

"Pam's brother says that Susie is the only girl he can stand to go skiing with, you know?" Paul said. "Last Sunday, he left his place in line at the lift just to come over and say hello to me. Man, do I rate!" He gave a nervous laugh. He was a freshman at Dartmouth.

"When I think of the way we believed the headaches were from studying for exams!" his mother said. "When I think of how we worried about whether she should wear glasses!"

"Let's just get Susie through the next twenty-four hours, that's all," Mr. Auerbach said.

"I forgot to tell you," Paul said. "Pam called up just before we left the house. She's awfully concerned about Susie. She's a damn nice kid. I like her brother, too."

His mother gave him a smile. "He's a nice boy, dear. And Pam's a lovely girl. Lovely." She tried to conceal a sudden onrush of tears by changing the position of her hands, of her purse. "For God's sake!" she said, at last. "Ernie, for God's sake!"

One of the post-operative strollers—a large man with powerful shoulders, and bald—came over to the Auerbachs. He had on an undersized Viyella tartan bathrobe, bagging out at

43

the seat, and loudly slapping, backless house slippers. He said, in a heavy Slavic-Jewish accent, "Was *I* scared silly on my admission to this hospital one week plus one day ago yesterday!"

The Auerbachs stiffened noticeably.

"Siegal," the large man said, extending his hand to Mr. Auerbach. "Nat Siegal."

Mr. Auerbach backed away slightly, but he took Mr. Siegal's hand and shook it. Paul did the same. The door of the room on the left at the end of the corridor was still open, and from this room came the raucous sounds of Rochester again being nagged by Jack Benny.

"Ah!" Mr. Siegal said, and with a wave of his hand he dismissed the patient in the room at the end of the corridor. "He's next to me. A big TV fan. Everybody is afraid of him."

The head floor nurse walked past without looking at any of them. She sneezed. Mr. Siegal gave the Auerbachs a significant look and shrugged. "Pneumonia, I hope not," he said, and, with an "Ah" and a wave of his hand, dismissed her. "You want to know why everybody is afraid of him?" He indicated the room of the big TV fan. "When all night long he has on Westerns? Shooting and shooting and shooting, with the door open? Because he is a prince! A real prince. A foreign potentate. And the whole hospital is afraid of him. Everybody must suffer because he's the prince!"

The Auerbachs gave feeble but authentic laughs. Mr. Siegal looked at them keenly. "Last night," he continued. "Bang! Bang! Bang! Until three o'clock in the morning. Finally, I'm asleep. So at five o'clock the floor nurse wakes me up. Why? To give me a sleeping pill!"

One end of Mr. Siegal's bathrobe belt was dragging on the floor. Paul picked it up and handed it to him.

44

"Much obliged." Mr. Siegal took a long cellophane-wrapped cigar from his bathrobe pocket and offered it to Mr. Auerbach. "Smoke?"

"Thanks, but not just now."

"Take it," Mr. Siegal said.

"Well—"

"It's from a gift box from a dear friend wishing me I should recover. He brings me a whole box of dollar-and-a-half cigars. So the doctor sees them. 'Siegal,' he says. 'No cigars!' So I give *him* the whole box. So he gives me two back, and he says, 'Here. Smoke it. *One*. Show you have will power with the other.' So here. Take it. I'm showing will power."

Mr. Auerbach took it.

The head floor nurse approached, carrying a bottle of clear liquid labelled "Dextrose—5% in Saline Intravenous." Mrs. Auerbach started.

"Nothing!" Mr. Siegal said as the head floor nurse took the bottle into Susan's room. "The way they scare people around here with their bottles! Bottles of this. Bottles of that. They put the bottles in the rooms to impress the visitors! I have become an expert on these matters in this hospital. Bottles! Ah!" Again he made the gesture of dismissal, this time at the door to Susan's room. "Listen, I don't mean to intrude, but I've been marching back and forth watching you. You're nice people. A fine family. I don't like to see you worry."

"You're very kind," Mrs. Auerbach said.

Susan had just asked Spencer, who was sitting in the arm-chair and smoking, if she would miss much of the semester at school.

"You Smith girls, you never change," Spencer said, with a laugh. "Hate to miss your classes? Or is it the skiing? Frankly,

45

I've always meant to take up skiing, but I never got around to it."

The girl on the bed reminded him of all the college girls and boys of his own Amherst days whose life he'd always wanted to be a part of. What he had thought was that eventually their ranks would open and he would be taken in. That hadn't happened. To this day, just thinking about those boys and girls, with their dates in fast convertibles, their hair blowing, made his throat tighten and go dry and his hands grow cold in apprehension. The feeling had never lifted for him. But this one—Susan Auerbach—was different. She didn't make him feel like an outsider. It was easy with her. His throat was neither tight nor dry. His hands were not cold. As he looked at her, he kept smiling. He felt happy. He said, "Do you go skiing a lot with your friends?"

"Oh, yes, but it's fun to go alone, too," Susan said. "Sometimes it's even better that way."

"Not much left of the skiing season," Spencer said.

"Oh, yes. March. Sometimes April."

"It always looks so easy, coming down those slopes," Spencer said.

"My mother here?"

"Right outside. I like your mother. Did she go to Smith, too?"

"Hunter."

"Frankly, Hunter's changed a lot since her day," he said.

"My father here? My brother?"

"Right here. I like your dad. He's got good taste in buildings. I like Paulie, too. Frankly, he's not callow, like a lot of Dartmouth boys. He seems to have real values."

She closed her eyes, but Spencer didn't notice. He gave another laugh, at what he was about to say. "Some of those

46

Indians! Frankly, our Jeffs, at Amherst, were what I guess you would call cool. I used to date a lot of Smith girls, being practically next door. Frankly, I've always thought Smith girls had it all over Vassar girls. I like Barnard girls, too. I understand that shorts are now *verboten* at Barnard."

Spencer liked to say that he could talk about almost anything with his patients. Name any subject and he had a little up-to-the-minute information on it, and an opinion. His feeling of relaxation deepened. He felt he was going great with Susan.

She opened her eyes. "Will I have a big scar?" she asked, looking at the ceiling. "Will it show?"

Spencer didn't hear, as often happened when he was absorbed in some of his own interests. "What about knickers at Smith?" he asked. "I hear they're going in for knickers and those big, bulky sweaters at Smith."

"Will I?" Susan asked.

"What?"

"Have a scar?"

"Oh. Nobody will be able to see a thing. It won't take long for your hair to grow back and cover it all up. What about trampolines? Are trampolines a thing at Smith?"

Susan had closed her eyes again.

"Susan?"

She didn't answer.

Spencer sat there and finished his cigarette. Regretfully, he got up and went out to the corridor. "Susan is a wonderful girl!" he said when he joined the Auerbachs. "I like her."

"Is she all right?" Mrs. Auerbach asked. "Is she awake? Can we see her?"

"Can we go in now, Dr. Fifield?" Mr. Auerbach asked.

47

Spencer took his time before saying anything. It was an old habit of his to pause when he was confronted with the need to respond in some way to the anxieties of others. It had become a kind of reflex. "My guess is that Susan is going to be fine," he said, at last. "Frankly, I'm sticking my neck out at this point, but that's what I think." He sniffed. Their Harvey Davis might not commit himself at this point, even in a qualified way. Neither would Phil Brody, in all probability. Spencer didn't mind taking chances. He was always ready to walk into touchy situations. He looked happily at each of the Auerbachs in turn. He took a package of cigarettes from his coat pocket and offered it around.

"Not right now," Mrs. Auerbach said. "We'd better go in and see her now."

"Don't you smoke?" Spencer asked Paul. "Good for you," he said as Paul shook his head. Spencer took a cigarette and lit it. "You're better off without it. Especially on the ski slopes." He inhaled deeply. "Susan and I talked a lot about skiing," he said, with a smile.

"How long can we stay with her?" Mrs. Auerbach asked.

Again, Spencer paused a bit longer than was necessary. "Oh, you can stay with her until she's ready to go, except when we do the spinal ta—" He stopped himself, after going far enough to get over clearly the name of the test to be done. Then he gave a small, contented sigh. "Susan understands everything," he said. "She's a very realistic person."

Paul coughed and shifted his feet. He put his hands in his pockets.

Spencer smiled at him. "A non-smoking cough?" he said, with a laugh. "It doesn't sound serious," he said to Mrs. Auerbach. He turned back to Paul. "Susan says you do a lot of skiing, too. . . . Susan wants very much to get well. Basically, she seems to have a very healthy set of values. I enjoy talking to her, quite frankly. Smith girls have it all over Vassar girls, in my humble opinion. I felt that way when I was up at Amherst, which is, you know, right near Smith. Amherst boys can't help but feel partial to Smith girls," he added, speaking in the manner of one insider to another.

Mrs. Auerbach held back from entering Susan's room. She frowned. "Dr. Fifield, you've told us everything, haven't you? You're not concealing anything?"

"Of course not." This time, the reply was quick and indignant. Spencer drew deeply on his cigarette. "We won't know the whole story until tomorrow morning, but we'll know the important thing tonight. You've got Burt Solender, the best surgeon you could possibly have, frankly, for the job. He does beautiful work. I've watched him operate many times. I've never seen anybody do such beautiful work. Harvey Davis would be the first to ask for Burt Solender. And, as I say, I think she'll be perfectly normal."

Spencer looked puzzled. Hadn't he *told* them he was sticking his own neck out? What more was there to say?"

"And she's not upset now, is she?" Mr. Auerbach asked.

"She's *fine*," Spencer said. "She's probably *asleep*. We were having a great discussion about Smith just before I left." He added quickly, to Paul, "You Indians still have all those milk-punch parties Sunday mornings?"

"Well, some of the guys do, I guess," Paul said.

"I know several people at Dartmouth," Spencer said. "Bo Sperling? Do you know him? He hangs out a lot at the Beef-eater." Spencer turned to Mr. Auerbach. "Bo's dad is in the construction business. One-family homes, in those West-chester development areas."

Mr. Auerbach nodded in an abstracted way and, with his wife, took a few steps toward Susan's door.

Spencer went on rapidly, "Bo's dad tells me that Bo and

49

some of the other boys now go in for attending classes in their bare feet. Jed Cooper?" he added, desperately. "Do you know Jed? I think Jed's a freshman, too."

Just then Mr. Nat Siegal came out of his room, the bathrobe belt again trailing on the floor. "Hello, *visitors!*" he called out to the Auerbachs. Spencer didn't pay any attention to Mr. Siegal, but the Auerbachs paused.

"Listen!" Mr. Siegal said breathlessly. "You want to know something terrific that just happened?"

Paul picked up the end of the bathrobe belt and handed it to Mr. Siegal.

"Much obliged," Mr. Siegal said. "Listen. I want to tell you nice people something. For me, one week plus one day ago yesterday everything was dark. Black. I didn't know what was going to take place. So tonight what happens? I call up my son. And my granddaughter is still up. She gets on the phone with me. Four years old. And she says, 'So long, Sammy—see you in Miami!' Four years old!"

Spencer looked to see how the Auerbachs would take what seemed to him a nervy interruption, considering the family's mood. To his surprise, their anxiety gave way to a look of pleasure.

"Oh, Mr. Siegal!" Mrs. Auerbach exclaimed. "How dear!"

"So you see?" Mr. Siegal said.

Spencer kept his glance averted from Mr. Siegal. He edged nearer to the Auerbachs, about to resume his talk. But the Auerbachs were giving their full attention to Mr. Siegal, and Spencer found that he couldn't talk any more. The Auerbachs and this Mr. Siegal were together. They had isolated him.

50

★ III ★

AT THE HAIRDRESSER'S, Annie Melvin was assigned to a stylist named Mr. Robert and to a manicurist named Molly, who also gave her a shampoo. Luxuriating in the posh atmosphere, she lay tilted back in a chair, her head over the basin, as Molly worked the suds through her hair.

"Take my advice," Molly said. "Take a Protein Rinse."

"O.K.," Annie said. "What is it?"

"Protein," Molly said. "Like milk. Eggs. Fish. Nourishment for the hair."

"O.K. I'll have it."

"With protein you get strong, healthy roots," Molly said.

Upright again after the Protein Rinse, Annie was turned around in her chair, and faced the mirror, waiting for Mr.

51

Robert. Annie, twenty-eight and delicately built, had dark eyes deep-set in a stubborn, small face. She had taken off her shell-rimmed eyeglasses, and couldn't see herself very clearly in the mirror.

Molly moved in alongside on a rolling footstool and started the manicure. "You got strong fingernails—healthy," Molly said. "You eat a lot of Jello?"

"Sometimes," Annie said.

Mr. Robert came over and gave her tangled mass of hair a disdainful survey. He was a handsome young man, with blond, neatly barbered hair.

"Jello is good for the fingernails," Molly said.

Annie watched Mr. Robert in the mirror. Poker-faced, he sprinkled wave-set lotion on her hair and combed it through.

"Carrots are good for the eyes," Annie said to Molly, who stopped sawing away with an emery board and looked at her. "My mother used to tell me that."

"Meat bones are good for the teeth," Molly said, starting to saw away again.

"How?" Mr. Robert said.

"They exercise the teeth," Molly said. "Also the gums."

"Like dogs?" Mr. Robert said.

"Like my father," Molly said. "He loved the bone from roast beef. Also from chickens." She smoothed the corners of Annie's fingernails. "My father never went to a dentist in his life," Molly said. "His outstanding feature was his smile."

"My dog won't go near a bone," Mr. Robert said. "He hates them."

"He always said the best part of the roast beef was the bone," Molly said.

"He's this Pekinese?" Mr. Robert said. He talked soft Southern, with a hushed, confiding drawl. "I cooked some special chicken livers for him this morning? He won't eat beef

52

liver. He's such a snob." He rolled a front curl over a large pink hair roller and looked fully at Annie for the first time. "Where you going tonight, honey?" he asked.

"To somebody's house for dinner," Annie said.

Mr. Frederick, who presided over the salon, came by and said gently, "Pull it back, Robert. *Pull* it."

Mr. Robert nodded and pulled Annie's hair back, working another curl over another roller. "Frederick is leaving tonight for Grosse Pointe," he said to Annie. "He's got this big coming-out party? He's doing all their hair? He's being flown out in a private plane." He yawned. "I didn't get a wink of sleep all night."

"You stay up late watching television?" Molly said. "It's bad for the back."

"My dog," Mr. Robert said. "All Pekinese snore. Mine makes more noise than five of my brothers. I'm the youngest of seventeen children. Whole bunches of us used to sleep in the same room down home, in Alabama? My father is a Baptist minister, and he loved children."

"I'm the oldest," Molly said. "Of five."

"What are you, honey?" Mr. Robert said to Annie.

"Next to the youngest of four," Annie said.

"Natural polish?" Molly said to Annie.

"Please," Annie said.

"I could tell," Molly said. "I can always tell when it's that."

A handsome lady walked past behind Mr. Robert and blew him a kiss in the mirror. He looked pleased. "Her family invented one of the freezer doodads that go in the icebox," he said softly to Annie. "Every time an icebox is sold, she gets money. Some people have all the luck."

"Is Frederick going to be the only passenger in the plane?" Molly said. "Like the last time?"

"They sent it up special for him," Mr. Robert said. "All the other guests are there now. They were flown in from the far corners of the world. It ought to be some party, for a coming-out party."

"Two dance orchestras," Molly said. "One a special Twist band."

Mr. Robert yawned again. "I've been trying for ages to get a coming-out party," he said. "All I ever got was a *bar mitzvah.*"

"I never went anyplace in an entourage," Molly said. "It would be nice to go like to India with Mrs. Kennedy."

"She had only one," Mr. Robert said. "The Shah's wife and royalty like that take twenty."

"At least you travel with actresses, with singers, at concerts and galas and balls and things like that," Molly said. "I mean, I never went to anything once."

"One of my clients gave a party for the Duke and Duchess of Windsor?" Mr. Robert said. "I had to come half an hour early. Everybody had to be there ahead of the Duke and Duchess."

"You always have to do special things for royalty," Molly said.

"All the ladies were expected to curtsy for the Duchess," Mr. Robert said. "They don't *have* to curtsy, the way they do for the Queen, but they do it because the Duke likes it?"

"What did *you* do?" Molly asked.

"I was in the other room, thank God," Mr. Robert said. "I always think I wouldn't give royalty the time of day, but when I'm up close, it gets me anyway, you know? Like when I was in Italy, and I saw the Pope, I felt really awed. I probably would have gone down on one knee or something like that for the Duchess."

"You don't *have* to," Molly said.

"You don't think you'll do it, but then it gets you and you do do it," Mr. Robert said. "You know?"

"If you're standing on the other side of the room and she comes in and you have your back to her or something like that, then you don't have to do it," Molly said.

"I went to this big party the other night," Mr. Robert said. "This man, the host, has so many paintings he gives you a catalogue of them the minute you step inside the door. I stayed in the bedroom. All the ladies kept coming in to see me, one by one? To get their hair combed? I was the most popular man at the party."

"They're putting special food on the plane taking Frederick to Grosse Pointe," Molly said. "I heard it was flown in from Maxim's. From Paris."

"All caviar tastes alike," Mr. Robert said. "This *bar mitzvah* was loaded with it. At the other party, the big one the other night, they kept trying to get me stoned. Every time they came in for a hair comb, they brought me another glass of champagne."

"How about the *bar mitzvah?*" Annie asked.

"The boy's parents took over a whole resort hotel for it," Mr. Robert said. "Grossinger's. It's this party given for boys when they get to be thirteen years old."

"What's the capacity of Grossinger's?" Annie asked. "How many people?"

"Thousands," Mr. Robert said. "Nobody who wasn't a guest of the *bar mitzvah* was admitted. The party lasted a whole weekend. I did the mother and a dozen relatives' hair. The champagne flowed." Mr. Robert yawned again. "That damn Pekinese."

"You spoil him," Molly said. "Give him a bone—it's good for his teeth and his nature, too."

"Champagne for thirteen-year-olds?" Annie asked.

"Of course," Mr. Robert said. "The idea of the *bar mitzvah* is to celebrate their becoming a man. I'm mad for all that kind of Grossinger food. I'm mad for kosher food." He started working on Annie's back curls.

"If you had to choose, which would you choose?" Molly asked. "Grossinger's or Maxim's?"

"I never let myself be driven into those kind of choices," Mr. Robert said.

Molly spread the last of the nail polish on and blew on it to make it dry quickly. "You go to a lot of big dinners," she said. "You're accustomed to rich food."

"I went to the 'Salute to Javits' dinner," Mr. Robert said. "He's a great man, and I adore his wife, but the salutes were very boring."

"Was that at Grossinger's, too?" Annie asked.

"At the Waldorf, honey," Mr. Robert said.

Mr. Frederick came over. "When we comb it out, we'll give her a sort of little cap effect, Robert," he said.

Mr. Robert nodded. "I make the best matzo balls in town," he said to Annie. "Mine are better than Grossinger's. First I buy the matzo meal. Then I take two eggs. I beat the whites and fold them in with it, the matzo meal. Then I add lots of butter—half a stick."

"Butter is very important for the skin," Molly said.

"Butter is very important in matzo balls," Mr. Robert said. "I mix it all up good, with water and salt, and pepper it up. Then I leave it in the icebox for two hours. Then you either make little balls, which I don't personally care for myself, or you just drop the batter a little at a time in the soup. With lots of carrots and celery. Peas are delicious wih matzo balls. My matzo-ball soup is better than Grossinger's. What kind of dinner party you going to tonight, honey?" he said to Annie as he fixed a hair net over his handiwork. He placed pads of tissue between her ears and the net, to protect her from the heat of the dryer.

"Sort of a family thing of a friend of mine," Annie said. "In an apartment on the upper East Side."

"I hope it isn't a birthday. Birthdays are the worst," Mr. Robert said.

"I don't know *what's* worst," Annie said.

Molly finished the manicure and disappeared in a rush. Mr. Robert switched on the dryer. The roar of the motor shut out all other sound, and Annie settled back in her chair, enjoying the detachment. After about ten minutes, the dryer was clicked off and the sounds of the salon returned sharply. Then she heard Mr. Robert drawling in her ear, "Lots of people put dill in matzo-ball soup, but I'm not fond of dill. I put parts of chicken in—wings and necks and all like that? The necks have lots of meat on them." He gave Annie a pat on the shoulder and turned the dryer back on.

★ **IV** ★

THE MAIN REASON Annie said yes when Spencer asked her to join him and his parents in their Passover Festival dinner was that she didn't have the courage to say no. She didn't want to hurt the feelings of any of them. Spencer's mother had a kind of wistfulness about her that made Annie want to be nice to her. And Spencer's father—a gentle, gloomy man who had been conditioned over a period of four decades to a you-first attitude toward his father-in-law, even with the latter dead—always made a big effort to be a joke-telling entertainer, in a way that made Annie's heart go out to him. So here she was pretending to be pleased, flattered, and happy about an invitation that she hardly had the strength to contemplate. But she couldn't stand the idea of Spencer's thinking that it was his *parents* she didn't want to be with.

Annie's own parents were dead, and it was such a little thing to do, to be nice to Mr. and Mrs. Fifield, especially since she had the evening free. It was a little thing to do for Spencer, too, who had been hanging around for a long time without much encouragement—a situation she felt guilty about. Spencer's face, on rare occasions, gave Annie some slight sign of wanting to be brought alive. But she knew that she was not the one to do it. Dr. Blauberman had decreed that she was suitable wife material, and Annie received, via Spencer, intermittent directives along these lines from Dr. Blauberman. After one particularly stimulating, Horizontal session with Dr. Blauberman, in fact, Spencer telephoned Annie early one morning, waking her from sleep, and said he had to see her at once, it was important. When they met, at the corner drugstore, he said, "Let's get married." He was so steamed up with Blauberman thoughts that he didn't see the look of panic on Annie's face. "We're alike—I went to Amherst, you went to Barnard," he said. "I've always wanted to marry a Barnard girl. Did you know that Dr. Blauberman's wife went to Barnard? A doctor should be married. I'm not intellectualizing as much as I used to, frankly. And I'm older than you. I want to be older than you. We'll have a quick, quiet wedding. With only your parents and mine."

"My parents are dead," Annie said. "You know they're dead."

Very often, Spencer did not catch what was being said to him. "Frankly, if it doesn't work, we can always get divorced," he said.

It was Annie's opinion that Dr. Blauberman was trying to unload Spencer on her, but she held her tongue. To herself she remarked that that was what came of having been such a patient listener to Spencer—all those complaints about his parents, his enthusiasm for his nearly eleven years of psycho-analysis with Dr. Blauberman and more to come, his tales of high adventure at Riverdale School, Amherst, the P. & S. medical school, and his three months in World War II on a cruiser in the Navy. In these long-drawn-out sagas Spencer presented himself cleanly framed against a background of well-heeled, Ivy League, fatuous, socially acceptable types— a group he was detached from and superior to but to which, he made it clear, he nevertheless damn well belonged. God knows what qualities Spencer and his analyst had endowed *her* with.

"Spencer, I'm sorry," she said. "But I *told* you. I'm in love with somebody else. Honest, I cross my heart, I hope to die, I'm in love with Josh Leonard."

"Dr. Blauberman doesn't believe you," Spencer said.

"Honest. Cross my heart. Hope to die."

The list of parental crimes against Spencer in Spencer's dossier, compiled and kept up to date with a big assist from his psychoanalyst, was a long one, and Spencer had played the record over and over and over again to Annie. She was bored with the record. What difference did it make at his age? After nearly eleven years of analysis, why not throw the record away?

"For crying out loud, Spencer," she would say, "*every-body's* parents did them in, one way or another. Saw it off, man." Annie enjoyed using beat talk. Her brother Mike, who was on the staff of the same hospital as Spencer, found it particularly annoying. Though she was fond of her brother, she saw no reason to let him censor her vocabulary, and she went right on using expressions that she had picked up in the Greenwich Village coffeehouse where she had taken a part-time job as a waitress. She had quit her job as a lab technician at the hospital because she could not throw off the sense she felt all around her of an attraction to sickness and death.

"You don't know," Spencer would say, insisting on playing the record. "Frankly, my mother has powerful masculine drives. *She* wants to be the doctor."

"So what? Give her a job as your receptionist in your office or something."

"Dr. Blauberman wouldn't approve, frankly. He's warned me she'll keep trying to take me over. It took me about ten years after I got out of the Navy to get away from her and move into my own apartment."

Then Spencer would dig into his complaint dossier and put on the record again: his mother had made him stay clean and had kept him from playing with other children; his mother had dominated his father; his mother's father had dominated Spencer's mother and father; his father was a big disappointment to Spencer's mother and everybody; his mother telephoned him every time she had a little heart palpitation; his mother used to make him cry when he was a little boy, and only then would she comfort him; his mother and father kept after him to have dinner with them at least once a week; and on and on and on. It was a long-playing record.

Spencer's parents were in their mid-sixties, but their faces were stamped with what Annie was sure was the expression they had worn in their early teens. Mrs. Fifield was nervous, jittery, a chain smoker, and eager to please. Mr. Fifield was uncertain, mild, still hopeful of winning a word of praise from the spirit of his father-in-law, and eager to please. Annie wanted to tell them not to worry about Spencer. Someday it would all be better. Someday Spencer would like them better than he did now. Their anxiety and general uneasiness with her and their efforts to show an interest in her that they didn't feel, and their simple overeagerness to please her, Spencer—anybody—made for an oppressive atmosphere. The moment she accepted Spencer's invitation, she began to feel a vaguely familiar downward, dreary pull at her insides. It was not the atmosphere to walk into at a festive time celebrating deliverance, freedom, and joy. But walk into it Annie did.

Annie, in addition to having her hair done, tried dressing up for the occasion in a way she thought Spencer's parents might like. You were supposed to put on new clothes for Passover. She bought new shoes—high-heeled black suède pumps with fashionably pointed toes—to wear instead of the old black ballet slippers that were part of her favorite costume. (With them she wore—day in and day out, when she was working and at other times as well—a dirndl skirt and a black jersey turtleneck blouse.) In a surge of high spirits because it was spring, she bought a décolleté, brightly flowered silk dress. Décolletage was a big issue with Spencer. Dr. Blauberman had informed him that girls who wore low-cut dresses were girls who were unafraid of being women. Seeing herself in the new dress and in the new shoes made her feel pretty good, just the same, when she looked in her full-length mirror. She gave her glasses—which were, as usual, blurred with an accumulation of fingerprints—a special, thorough wiping before putting them on. Too bad her brother Mike couldn't see her now, looking so solidly middle-class, and observing the holiday tradition of new clothes. He would approve so energetically of her going to a home dinner —and a Passover dinner, at that. Her brother put in a good

62

deal of time worrying about her unsettled place in the social scheme and her going around with what he called crazy beatnik jazz musicians. He suspected that she might even be considering getting married to Josh, a jazz pianist who worked nights at a Village spot called the Zero Inn. Her brother had his own long-playing record. Well, going to the Fifields' was better than going to a Passover dinner at the home of one of her unclose relatives, all of whom assumed that she smoked marijuana.

"Delman's?" Spencer asked, indicating the shoes, and without waiting for the answer (I. Miller's) he commented favorably on the dress.

Annie felt herself sinking, and she began to brace herself to face the next hours.

Spencer's parents lived in a small four-room apartment in a prewar-rental apartment house on the upper East Side. Heading for it in Spencer's white convertible, Annie noticed that he drove more unevenly than usual, speeding to make lights, then absent-mindedly slowing down. It was a warm, humid evening. A light drizzle was in the air. And Spencer was trying, as he did every once in a while, to persuade her to return to her job at the hospital.

"Coffeehouses!" he said. "What's in it for you?"

"The Freeplace?" she said. "I love it. It's the opposite of the hospital. It's not depressing. I get a *lot* out of it."

"What?"

"It makes me feel good. It's wonderful just standing around and listening to jazz records. I love serving *espressos*."

"Being a *waitress?*" He went through a red light and turned up Park Avenue.

"I love giving people things to eat and drink. I love it. I

get a kick out of learning to hold three cups and saucers in one hand. I even love getting tips." It was the furthest she'd ever gone in trying to tell Spencer anything.

"You're way out, kid," he said, with a sniff, in a knowing, beat-talk manner. The car skidded as he sped around a taxi. "I hate all taxi-drivers," he said. "All taxi-drivers try to push you around if you let them get away with it." He gave a deep sigh. Keeping one hand on the wheel, he put the other one at the back of Annie's neck. She stiffened. "I'm glad you're coming tonight. Frankly, my mother is very mad at me. She called me up at midnight last week. I was dog-tired. She kept me on the phone for half an hour, complaining about her heart. I told her she has her own doctor, why call *me?* I had to hang up on her. I haven't talked to her all week."

"What about her heart?"

"What do you mean?"

"Does she have heart trouble?"

"Oh, she had mild coronary symptoms a couple of years ago. Frankly, I think she's strong as a horse. Dr. Blauberman says her complaints are her way of holding on to me. She just won't let go." Spencer sniffed again.

"Maybe she just wants sympathy. All you have to do is *talk.*"

"No," Spencer said. "She keeps making demands. She could learn from you. You don't make demands."

"You're wrong, man! I'm terribly demanding. Really."

"It's a very common thing in mothers with masculine drives," he said, showing no sign of having heard Annie.

"Well, why shouldn't they look for some satisfaction in their sons? Or in their daughters? After all. Who decided it was such a crime, anyway?"

64

Spencer was still totally absorbed in his own theories. "I hung right up on her," he said.

"Gosh, Spencer. You're her only child. Her only son. The doctor. The magician. The anchor. She depends on you. You can fix anything." Sinking, sinking, sinking. Annie tried to keep her tone light.

"That reminds me of a Jewish-doctor joke," Spencer said. At last. She had connected.

"This old Jewish mother is running frantically along the beach at the ocean. She's got her arms stretched out to the water, and she's yelling, 'Help! Help! My son the doctor is drowning!'"

Annie laughed. Her feeling of oppression deepened.

Mr. and Mrs. Fifield together met them at the door, barely one second after they had rung the bell. Both kissed Annie with the overenthusiasm of parents trying much too hard to be more than friendly. Annie was touched by the kisses and, even more, by the false enthusiasm. Everybody commented on how well everybody else looked.

"I'm tired," Spencer said. "That damn Mrs. Stone woke me up at three in the morning to ask if it was all right to take an extra sleeping pill."

"Couldn't she sleep?" Mrs. Fifield asked. The Fifields had trouble connecting with each other as well as with other people.

Mrs. Fifield didn't seem a bit angry about her son's hanging up on her. She and her husband were all dressed up, and smelled of tangy after-shave lotion and freshly applied perfume. Mr. Fifield, in a crisply pressed dark suit and blue-and-white polka-dot bow tie, looked like Spencer's older brother—the same even features, the same shade of brown hair in the same crew-cut style, but with a more receding hairline. He had a mild, apologetic face that faintly suggested the evasiveness and inertness of Spencer's. Mrs. Fifield was short and thin, with bleached-blond hair in puffs over her ears—the "cootie-garage" style of the nineteen-twenties. Her face was deeply lined and pale, and her expression conveyed that she was one hundred per cent grateful for Spencer's presence. Her voice was pleasantly hoarse, and she gave a hoarse little giggle as a kind of end flourish to almost every sentence. She talked fast and too much, and was too ready to say everything the What's Polite book called for. She had on a white lace blouse and narrow purple silk skirt that Spencer had brought her recently as a gift from the Virgin Islands.

They went into the living room, immaculate and homey, its forty-year-old furniture decoratively tacked and topped here and there with white lace doilies. The room was dominated by a large color-television set with a monster screen and a panel of twenty-fourth-century dials—also a present from Spencer, who had obtained the set, at a considerable discount, from Hiram Stone. There was an old baby-grand piano in the room, the top crowded with Fifield photographs—the wedding of Mr. and Mrs., forty years ago; the glamour-profile, dreamy-eyed photo of Mrs., forty-one years ago, wearing her hair in the same "cootie-garage" style; Spencer on the occasion of his graduation from college, the mortarboard adjusted mathematically to perfect position and resting well up on the top of his head. There were small cut-glass dishes placed here and there—one with peanuts, one with chocolate candies, one with white square mints—and a bowl of walnuts with a complex teakwood nutcracker, a present from Spencer from the days of the war.

"Sit down, sit down, sit down," Mr. Fifield said cordially. They sat.

"We won't have a drink, because we've got wine with the dinner—unless you really want a drink," Mrs. Fifield said.

"I need a drink," Spencer said.

"You want a drink?" his father asked him.

"Let's have a drink," Spencer said.

"Would you like a drink, Annie?" Mrs. Fifield asked.

"I'd just as soon wait for the wine."

"You're like me," Spencer's mother said. "I don't drink. All I take is a tiny sip of wine. Even that makes me dizzy."

"Oh, I like a drink before dinner sometimes," Annie said.

"What is there to drink?" Spencer asked. He cracked a walnut and threw the nut meats into his mouth.

"We've got Manischewitz wine," Spencer's father said. "Very sweet."

"Do you really want a drink?" Spencer's mother asked.

"Manischewitz," Annie said. "What fun. I haven't tasted that dear old sweet, sticky Manischewitz in five years, I'll bet."

"Frankly, I prefer Mogen David to Manischewitz," Spencer said. "You got any Scotch? Annie, Scotch-and-soda?"

"Sure," Annie said, and then added hastily, "That is, if you're having one anyway."

"You're like me," Mrs. Fifield said. "I can't drink, either." Well, what could you do if she just didn't catch what was being said to her?

"We don't have any Scotch," Mr. Fifield said. "I think we've got vodka. Or maybe it's gin."

"Herb never drinks, either," Mrs. Fifield said.

"If you don't have any Scotch, I don't want anything," Spencer said. He scooped up some peanuts and tossed them into his mouth.

"I could run out for some Scotch," his mother said. "Or Daddy could."

"Naw," Spencer said. "Maybe I'll just have a quick jigger of vodka."

"We don't have time for a drink anyway. I don't want the soup to get cold," Mrs. Fifield said. After a pause, she lit a cigarette and inhaled deeply. "Spencer tries to get me to stop smoking, but last time I tried I lasted exactly thirty-two hours." She gave a little hoarse giggle, inhaled nervously, and let out a stream of smoke that blurred the piano and its entire set of photographs for several seconds.

"Thirty-two and a half," Mr. Fifield said.

Mrs. Fifield gave another hoarse giggle of self-reproach.

"You smoke too damn much," Spencer said. Abandoning the fancy nutcracker, he cracked two walnuts, one against the other, and said, "I think I'll wait till I can get some decent Scotch."

"Herb, are you sure we don't have a bottle of Scotch?" Mrs. Fifield said, turning to her husband. "From last Christmas? The present from—who was it?"

"They sent the vodka," Mr. Fifield said.

"I'd just as soon have some vodka," Annie said. "If you're having some, Spencer."

"I don't want the soup to get cold," Mrs. Fifield said. "We'd better go in and start. You came a little late. If you want a drink, you can have it at the table, if you really need it that much. Is it raining outside?"

"Frankly, I didn't notice," Spencer said.

They all got up and made for the kitchen.

"It's just starting to drizzle," Annie said.

"I hope it keeps up," Mr. Fifield said. "Ask me why."

"We'll skip the drink," Spencer said. "I'm starved."

"Why?" Annie asked Mr. Fifield.

"So it won't come *down*." He chuckled.

"Herb and his jokes," Mrs. Fifield said. "He always kept Papa in stitches. Remember, Spencer? The way he always kept Grandpa in stitches?"

"Next time, get Mogen David wine," Spencer said.

The table was set in a small dining nook next to a window in the kitchen. The kitchen was gleaming and spotless. Standing by the stove was a disgruntled middle-aged woman who was wearing a white short-sleeved smock and heavy black oxfords with square, low heels.

"Mrs. Browning offered to stay and give me a hand with the serving," Mrs. Fifield said, throwing a short giggle in the woman's direction. "I get so tired these days myself. I don't think my heart is what it used to be, Spencer."

"If you really think there's something wrong with your heart, go to see Joey Chankin. He's your doctor," Spencer said.

"The table looks lovely," Annie said, feeling like Pollyanna.

"Very nice," Spencer said.

"I'd never have been able to do it without Mrs. Browning."

Mrs. Browning didn't flick an eyelash. "Don't let the soup get to you lukewarm," she said.

The table looked better than lovely. A white embroidered cloth—present from Spencer from Puerto Rico. Heavy old-fashioned silver, solid, shining gloriously. Silver salt and pepper shakers—gift from Spencer from Mexico. Silver candelabra, two candles at each end of the table. Centerpiece featuring fresh sweet peas, freesias, and daisies. China decorated with golden threads in a pattern of roses. The candles were burning, and their light flickered against the silver. It was sweet. It was beautiful. Annie's mouth felt dry. She felt a flush of heat rush to her face. Her glasses were steaming.

69

She wanted to cry. Mrs. Fifield must have been planning that table for days. Annie looked at the three Fifield faces, each sunk into a mold of self-concern. If only she could feel something for Spencer. If only she could accept the challenge of his numbness, his coldness, his deadness, his plea. In other words, if only she were someone else. It would be nice to make the Fifields happy.

"Sit down, sit down, sit down," Mr. Fifield was saying.

Annie sat down across from Mrs. Fifield, who had her back to the kitchen, and with Spencer on her left, Mr. Fifield on her right. She turned around and looked at the window. A freshly laundered and starched white organdie café curtain blew gently out from the window. On the sill were half a dozen potted plants of various kinds. Spencer had once told Annie that his mother washed the leaves of her house plants morning and night. The plants were so clean they looked shellacked.

"I love a kitchen with a window," Annie said. "It's unusual in New York."

"They don't build them this way any more," Mr. Fifield said.

"It's worth holding on to, the rent you pay here," Spencer said. "It leaves you free to have it and still do anything else you like in the country."

"We always figured Spencer might take it over someday, because we have the summer house in Jersey," Mrs. Fifield said, giving Annie a significant look.

"I don't want it," Spencer said. "Someday I'm going to have a town house. I've always wanted one of those old town houses on the East Side somewhere. Like Grandpa's."

"I prefer an apartment in the city," Annie said. "I like a house in the country or at the beach."

70

The others gave no sign of interest in her preferences as to dwellings.

"Here, Herb." Mrs. Fifield handed a round white silk skull-cap to her husband and another one to Spencer. "We're not very Orthodox, but Grandpa always liked to have us observe the holidays," Mrs. Fifield said, with another giggle, to Annie.

Spencer was looking at a tape sewn into the inside of the skullcap, and read aloud, " 'Souvenir of the Marriage of Miss Linda Beth Weinbaum to Dr. Stanley Stephen Klippenberg, July 4, 1957, The Plaza, New York City.' " He put the skull-cap on the back of his head.

"We all attended Linda Weinbaum's wedding," Mrs. Fifield said. "It was a lovely affair."

"It cost a fortune," Mr. Fifield said.

"Frankly, I like S. S. Klippenberg, but I'd rather have the money," Spencer said.

"S. S. goes to a lady psychoanalyst," Annie said. "S. S. told me that's how he learned what makes what he calls 'a real woman.' "

"S. S. has opened up a lot since he went into treatment," Spencer said.

"Linda was a lovely person," Mrs. Fifield said. "She went to Vassar. A Vassar girl. She just had a baby. A boy."

"Old man Weinbaum set up a trust fund of a hundred and fifty thousand dollars for the baby," Mr. Fifield said.

O Linda Weinbaum! Why couldn't I have been you? If only another Linda Weinbaum would come their way!

"I hate Vassar girls," Spencer was saying. "They all have a mustache."

"Mrs. Fifield," Mrs. Browning said, from the stove. "You want the soup?"

71

"Not yet." Mrs. Fifield stood up, a little paper-covered booklet containing the Passover service in her hand. "We'll read fast," she said, handing similar booklets to the others at the table. "These are put out by the wine company. I don't know what ever happened to those wonderful little books Grandpa used to have—the ones with the red covers. . . . I'm supposed to light the candles and then read over them, but the candles are already lit." She cleared her throat and looked self-consciously at her son and then at her husband. She read the title, " 'The Kindling of the Festival Lights.' " Then she continued, reading fast, " 'This is the festival of Passover, a time of happiness and rejoicing, of celebration and of cheer. Its flame of freedom has never been quenched; its brightness has never been dimmed. As a symbol of God's eternal light, our beacon and our goal, we kindle these festival candles and say—' They have this part in Hebrew, and then they have the way to say the Hebrew words in English letters, lucky for me." Mrs. Fifield giggled and continued, " 'Boruch atto adonoy elohenu melech—' "

"Isn't that supposed to be read by a man?" Spencer interrupted.

"Grandpa always said a girl is supposed to recite the blessing over the candles," his mother said.

"Annie should read, frankly," Spencer said. "She's the girl."

Annie's hand shook so much she had trouble holding the booklet steady. She felt the new silk print dress clinging damply to her back. "Oh, no," she said, to Spencer's suggestion. "I couldn't pronounce the words." Even if she had wanted to read, she couldn't have kept her voice steady. The sound of those ancient ceremonial words—just barely familiar—in that Fifield setting was overwhelming. The way Mrs. Fifield looked as she read! So eager to please the heavens!

The face of Shirley Temple had probably never shone with more innocence.

"The soup?" Mrs. Browning called out firmly.

"That's enough," Mr. Fifield said, suddenly taking charge. "I'll speed things up." Mrs. Fifield sat down, and Mr. Fifield filled their glasses with the Manischewitz wine. Holding up his glass, he directed them to hold up theirs. Holding the booklet in his other hand, he quickly read from it, " '*Boruch atto adonoy elohenu melech ho'olom bore p'ri haggofen*. Blessed art Thou, O Lord our God, Ruler of the world, Creator of the fruit of the vine. (All drink the first cup of wine.)' O.K. Everybody drink."

They drank.

"O.K.?" Mrs. Browning called out.

"At least, let's have the Four Questions," Mrs. Fifield said, looking disappointed. "They're asked by the youngest at the table."

"I'm starved," Spencer said. "Let's ask them later."

"Grandpa always enjoyed your asking the Four Questions," Mrs. Fifield said.

"Annie's the youngest, but I'll make it faster," Spencer said, and, rushing the words, he read, "Why is this night different from all other nights? On all other nights we eat either leavened or unleavened bread; on this night, why only unleavened? On all other nights, we eat all kinds of herbs; on this night, why only bitter herbs? On all other nights, we do not dip the herbs even once; why on this night do we dip them twice? On all other nights, we eat either sitting or leaning; on this night why do we eat in a leaning position only?' Now I'll read for all the children who are supposed to give the answers," Spencer went on. " 'This night is different from all other nights because by this Seder service we recall our deliverance from Egypt, the house of bondage. We eat only unleavened bread tonight because when our ancestors left Egypt they were in so great a hurry that there was not time to prepare the ordinary bread out of a dough that has to leaven. So they made a thin bread instead, out of unleavened dough that would bake quickly. We eat only bitter herbs tonight to remind ourselves of the bitter time our people had in Egypt before God delivered us.' I'm skipping here to save time." Spencer turned some pages and read on, " 'Tonight we eat in a leaning position because tonight each Jew is like a king and his house is his palace; because tonight our slavery is ended and we celebrate this Festival of Passover as free men, thanking God for everything that He has done for us.' " Spencer stopped reading and lit a cigarette.

"O.K. *now?*" Mrs. Browning asked.

"Now is fine, Mrs. Browning," Mrs. Fifield said stiffly, turning her head in recognition of the stove.

O Lord our God, Ruler of the world, Creator of the fruit of the vine, save me, save me. . . . Annie felt herself slipping toward the Fifields. Something was grabbing at the general area of her heart. And she kept feeling more and more depressed.

"This is a hell of a Seder," Spencer said. He sipped at his second glass of wine. "Wine-company prayer books. Souvenir skullcaps. And, frankly, a few other details I won't mention. Grandpa must be turning over in his grave."

"That's no way to talk," his mother said, looking hurt. "It's just the idea of observing the holiday, that's all." She turned to Annie. "Was your family religious?"

"My mother was, rather," Annie said. "My father considered himself an agnostic. He—"

Mrs. Fifield interrupted. "Papa and Mama were both very religious. They tried to pass it on to Spencer."

74

Well, Mrs. Fifield had looked out momentarily, anyway. The family capacity for hearing was limited, and that was all there was to it. Mrs. Fifield's face was still turned toward Annie, however, as though that in itself signified polite interest.

Annie tried hard to think of something—anything—in her own history that would tie her to the Fifields. Some nice, juicy atavistic reminiscence. The Passover supper at some shadowy aunt's house, perhaps, where she had sipped red wine and become drunk at the age of seven or eight—or was it nine or ten? That wouldn't do. Her mother working in the kitchen, honey cake baking in the oven, sending out the sweet aroma of home? The spiciness, tantalizing, of fish cooking on the stove? That wouldn't do, either. It had never felt like this. It had more in common with her jazz-playing friends than it had with the Fifields.

The soup was delicious, aromatic—hot chicken soup, with matzo balls as light as air. Not like those golf balls you got in restaurants. Probably even better than Mr. Robert's. Fatless chicken soup, the drink of Jewish goddesses. Then the chicken. Perfect. As good as her mother's. Flaky, tender, light, and smelling of the soup, not of chicken. It was classic Jewish cooking of the highest order, all right. Spencer was very subdued during the meal, concentrating on his food and saying little. The wine was friendly and sweet to the tongue. Passover wine—the sweetest wine, most ridiculous wine of all wines. Spencer and his father refilled their glasses with it several times. Annie's eyes grew heavy after her second glass. Mrs. Fifield, true to her word, controlled her drinking to abstinence after the first sip. Mrs. Browning, deadpan and disdainful, filled the plates and replenished them. It grew warm in the kitchen. The breeze that had been coming in through the window had died down, and the white organdie

75

curtain now hung still. Spencer suggested that he and his father take off their jackets. Mrs. Fifield said it was all right with her, if Annie didn't mind, and gave a furtive glance in the direction of Mrs. Browning. The men took off their jackets and sat down again in their shirtsleeves. They looked touching—both slightly round-shouldered, human, their shirts smelling of laundry starch. Mrs. Fifield lit a cigarette. Mr. Fifield got up to get her an ashtray and swayed with the wine.

"Herb always gets drunk on Passover wine," Mrs. Fifield said. "Remember the way Grandpa used to kid him?"

"I saw a house in the East Sixties recently that looked just like Grandpa's house," Spencer said.

"I'm all right, Sonny," Mr. Fifield said to Spencer, with a weak smile. He handed his wife the ashtray. "Fella came into my office yesterday and told me a new Jewish joke," he said, taking his seat again. "This rabbi's wife dies, and the day of the funeral the rabbi keeps crying and beating his breast and wailing and refusing to be consoled or comforted. When all the relatives come back from the cemetery to the rabbi's house, they look all over for him. All over the house. He's gone. The relatives run all over the neighborhood hysterically, searching for him. Finally, they come back to the rabbi's house and go up to the attic, and there, on an old bed, hidden under the quilts, they find the rabbi, with the maid. 'Rabbi! What's the matter with you? Rabbi!' they cry to him. And the rabbi gives a shrug and asks, 'In my grief, do I know what I'm *doing*?' "

There was a round of self-conscious laughter.

"That's an old one," Spencer said. "I heard that one way back at Riverdale. I heard a funny one the other day. About three Jewish mothers. They meet on Fifth Avenue, and they're boasting to each other about their sons. One mother

76

says that her son is a very successful lawyer who does every-thing for her—bought her a mink coat, gave her a new co-op apartment, sent her to Palm Beach for the whole winter, and comes to see her every Saturday night. The second mother says, 'That's nothing. *My* son owns a chain of shoe stores and a lot of real estate, and he gave me a limousine with a chauf-feur to drive me all around, wherever I want to go, and he takes me to lunch at the Four Seasons twice a week.' The third mother says, 'That's nothing. Listen. Have *I* got a son? Five times a week, you know what he does? He goes to a doctor, lies down on a couch, and he talks only about *me*.' "

This one got a fair laugh, and Spencer seemed to feel better. "I wish I didn't have to go back to the hospital to-night," he said as Mrs. Browning placed cut-glass dishes of cooked prunes and apricots before them.

"Tonight?" Mrs. Fifield looked from Spencer to Annie. "Can't you take tonight off and stay here?"

"Impossible. I've got to see a patient. Very sick. Got to make some tests." He lit a cigarette, inhaled deeply, and let out a thick stream of smoke.

"Can't you do it tomorrow?"

"Tonight," Spencer said. "I don't know how long it'll take."

"I'll come with you," Annie said quickly.

There was a brief, smoky silence at the table. Mrs. Brown-ing poured the coffee, and then served up slices of frothy-looking spongecake.

"We promised to call up Cousin Bonnie," Mrs. Fifield said, finally, putting out her cigarette.

"My cousin in Bridgeport," Spencer said to Annie. "She just got into Bennington. Well," he said, reconsidering his decision to leave, "I'll hang around for a while, and we'll call her."

"We're supposed to congratulate her," Mrs. Fifield said,

with her giggle. "Can you believe it, little Bonnie now a Bennington girl? She's Spencer's first cousin," she said to Annie. "My sister's girl. A beautiful child. She was the most beautiful child you've ever seen. Last month, she won the Miss Brass Hardware of Bridgeport beauty contest. I'm so relieved, Spencer. Uncle Harry thought Bennington would hold it against her."

Spencer drank a fresh glass of wine. "My mother is nuts about Cousin Bonnie."

Mr. Fifield started from a semi-doze. "Bonnie's a beautiful girl," he said, and yawned. He took another glass of wine.

"I feel toward Bonnie as I would toward my own daughter," Mrs. Fifield said. "I take pride and joy in everything she does."

"When Cousin Bonnie is on the scene, we all take a back seat," Mr. Fifield said.

"Especially me," Spencer said, and sniffed. He continued to pay tribute, excitedly, to Bonnie. "She's the smartest and toughest kid I've ever known," he said. "She gets anything out of anybody. Anything she wants. And she knows exactly what she wants."

"Miss Brass Hardware of Bridgeport. Pretty good, eh, Sonny?" Mr. Fifield asked.

Spencer sniffed.

"The way she handled Bennington—their administration officer!" Mrs. Fifield said. "Her mother told me she had them eating out of her hand."

"The way she handles her boy friends!" Mr. Fifield put in.

"All her boy friends are either Princeton or Yale, and some Amherst Jeffs, I'm glad to say," Spencer said. "The way she handles those Jeffs!" He shook his head in wonder and admiration. He looked miserable.

78

Cousin Bonnie was giving Annie a swift pain. "Why does she have to *han*dle everybody?" she asked. "Does everybody need handling?"

None of the Fifields heard her question.

"She's coming to New York next week," Mrs. Fifield said. "I'm taking her shopping."

Spencer stood up from the table.

"Spencer has always been a little jealous of Bonnie," Mr. Fifield said.

"I love to take her shopping with me," Mrs. Fifield said. "She's so beautiful everybody turns to look at us. . . . Where are you going, Spencer?"

"To the hospital."

"But you said you'd wait till we called up Bonnie."

"Can't wait," Spencer said. "I've got a coronary to look in on. A sixty-one-year-old woman. Never had a bit of trouble. Suddenly she calls me in the middle of the night. Upset stomach. Chest pains. Bam! A massive coronary." Putting on his jacket, he said, "She probably won't last the week." He looked at Annie. "Coming? You can wait in the waiting room. I can come out every now and then to see you."

Mrs. Fifield's face was gray. She sat with her hands at her sides. She was abstracted. "Why not stay?" she asked, without energy, of Annie.

Annie looked at Mr. Fifield. He smiled at her blearily. "Stay with us," he said.

Annie felt trapped. Her new shoes with the too pointed toes were pinching her feet. It was hot and stuffy here. She couldn't draw a deep breath. She told the Fifields she'd love to stay and help call up Cousin Bonnie.

Spencer headed for the door. Neither Mr. nor Mrs. Fifield looked up to see him go.

"Got a cigarette, Herb?" Mrs. Fifield asked her husband in a low voice.

Mr. Fifield took out a fresh package of cigarettes, and, fumbling to undo the red band of cellophane tape, called out, "Take care, Sonny," into space.

O Linda Beth Weinbaum, why couldn't you have been me?

★ V ★

ANNIE was wiping off one of the tables in the Freeplace with a wet cloth when she looked up and saw Spencer walk in. With him were his friends Lester Greenthal and Julius Karp.

"Long time no see," Spencer said, grabbing her at the back of the neck in his finest junior-prom style.

"Two weeks," Annie said. Since Spencer was the only unmarried doctor in his medical circle, Annie had accompanied him to the your-turn-our-turn dinner parties that made up the routine social life of his colleagues and their wives, but it got her down when he continued his pretense that he and she were a team, on the verge of getting married.

"Hey, Annie kid, long time no see," Julius Karp said. He was Spencer's accountant.

81

"You going to feed us?" Lester Greenthal said to her. He had been Spencer's boyhood friend and was now his attorney. A bald, tensely good-natured fellow, Lester always looked to Annie as though he expected everybody to make him walk the plank. Both friends were about six feet two, and hovered over Spencer solicitously. Annie was glad when they sat down. When they were standing, she got dizzy trying to look up at them.

Spencer took an inventory of her clothes, and his attention settled on her mohair turtleneck sweater. "Lord and Taylor sweater bar?" he asked.

"Jax," Annie said, without interest.

"Don't forget," Spencer said to her now, with his two friends looming over him like parental giants, even when all three men were seated. "We have this big affair next month at the Plaza. S. S. and Linda Beth are celebrating their fourth wedding aniversary. Did you get your new formal?"

"I have to work, man!" Annie said. Spencer had never asked her to go to the Klippenbergs' anniversary party with him. As usual, he took it for granted both that she knew he wanted her to go with him and that she *was* going with him. That was part of the team act.

"Formal, hey, Annie kid?" Julius asked, beaming secret knowledge at her. In his own way, he led a unilateral team life with her that was more mysterious than Spencer's. As Annie saw it, Spencer liked to have Julius around him because Julius did his best to imitate him, but did not succeed.

"I'm terrible at those parties," Annie said.

"Don't worry about the new formal, *dear*," Spencer said. He said "dear" with a husbandly tone that, Annie thought, could indicate to an audience that the relationship was so deeply in the groove that he had reached the point of being

82

able to use the word and simultaneously make fun of it. As always, he was floundering around amid the accoutrements and vocabulary of love, without understanding what love itself was. Hence the convoluted "dear"; hence the team act; hence an endless number of other things. Spencer had even been able to propose marriage without realizing that his words might lead to a fateful action, or that love and marriage might have some bearing on each other.

Annie had introduced Spencer to other girls, hoping that he would become interested in them. Spencer merely included them in the audience for the team act, and then tried to demonstrate his loyalty and his faithfulness to her by tearing into the other girls. For example, Annie had introduced him to Victoria Russell, one of her Barnard classmates, who was working part time as an actress in a television soap opera.

"Isn't Victoria sweet?" Annie said later.

"Frankly, I don't like her," Spencer said. "I think she's a nymphomaniac."

"Victoria?" Annie asked. "You just *met* her. How can you tell?"

"The way she sat down so close to me," Spencer said. "That dress."

"I thought you *liked* décolleté dresses," Annie said.

"I don't care," Spencer said. "I don't like her. She's a nymphomaniac!"

Annie was a flop as Cupid.

"What about *us?*" Spencer said to her on that same occasion. "How about coming home with me tonight? It's time I had a relationship with some emotional content in it."

"Spencer, I can't," she said. "I'm in love with another man."

Spencer's blunt invitation didn't make her feel angry. It

83

was so earnest, and, besides, it was his idea of a gesture that had something to do with what you were supposed to feel. His mind was packed with all kinds of specialized information. He filled his head with odd facts, and from the people he knew—including Dr. Blauberman—he soaked up a multitude of ideas about feelings. There wasn't a human feeling that he hadn't learned to label or interpret or explain—especially other people's feelings. But what, or where, were his own? He had never found out. Spencer did not know what love was. His friends and his analyst were able to give him rules, regulations, definitions, directions, admonitions, boos, and cheers, and Spencer memorized them all very carefully, but it did not bring him any closer to the thing itself.

Whenever Spencer dropped in on Annie at the coffeehouse, he seemed to assume that she had been standing by during the interval between his visits, and that it had been filled, in her case, as in his own, with nothing.

Lester and Julius were giving the Freeplace menu a critical survey.

"Wow! Thirty-five cents for a plain ordinary *espresso!*" Lester said.

"Eighty-five cents for plain ordinary Genoa salami! Hey, Annie kid?" Julius said.

Spencer had told Annie that both Lester and Julius had deep-seated fears that their money was going to be taken away from them. "Frankly, Les is worse than Julie," Spencer had said. "Les once owed me a fifteen-dollar bill for six months because he wouldn't touch what he calls his principal."

Annie took their orders. All three wanted Genoa salami and provolone with Bermuda onion on pumpernickel. And three Caffè Royals—hot *espresso* with vanilla ice cream and whipped cream. Three cast-iron stomachs. When she brought them what they had ordered, Spencer urged her to sit with them. It wasn't too busy in the Freeplace. She looked over to the manager, and he gave her the O.K. She'd be through soon anyway, and then, as she did almost every night, she'd go over to the Zero Inn, a few blocks away, to meet Josh. She was impatient to hear his new trio again. After a couple of years of playing solo at the Zero Inn, Josh had just formed a trio with a colored drummer named Patrick Montrose and a white clarinettist, Ephraim Samuels; they all wore gray caps when they played. The cap-wearing had been initiated by the clarinettist. The sight of the trio, not to mention the sound, entranced Annie.

Annie got herself a cinnamon-stick *espresso* and sat down next to Spencer. Julius was telling the others about the psychoanalyst whom Dr. Blauberman had shunted him onto because he had a full house and couldn't take Julius on himself. The doctor was Samm Ascher.

" 'Samm' with a double 'm,' " Julius said. "Don't you think that's sort of pretentious?"

"If Dr. Blauberman thinks you should go to him, you should go," Spencer said.

"I'd much rather go to Dr. Blauberman, with you and Les," Julius said. "I'd be much more confident."

Julius's marriage had just broken up. Spencer had advised both Julius and his wife to go into treatment immediately to find out why. So far, only Julius had acted on the advice. Julius's wife's name was Jean, and they had a two-year-old boy, Hugh. Their towels were monogrammed with satin "J"s in genuine London script. On Hugh's second birthday, Jean had told Julius that it was all over. All they had together, she had said—and he had told Spencer, who had told Annie—was Hugh and the towels. So she was going to get a divorce. Julius had made arrangements for the divorce. He had made arrangements to go into psychoanalysis with Dr. Samm Ascher, come September. He had made arrangements to take half of the towels. And Annie now learned that he had just made arrangements to go to Europe to recover from it all. He was going with Lester, on a special chartered flight, with the Bakery Owners Association of New York. Five countries in eighteen days for three hundred and forty dollars, round trip, not including room and board. Not bad.

"They're going to Copenhagen," Spencer told Annie, grabbing the back of her neck with one hand and the salami-cheese-onion-on-pumpernickel with the other. "Copenhagen," he repeated, as if the city had some special significance.

"Swell," Annie said. "I've never been to Copenhagen."

"Denmark," Spencer said, with more emphatic significance.

"Denmark, hey, Annie kid?" Julius said, lifting his eyebrows à la Groucho Marx. What it was she was supposed to share with Julius she could never make out.

"Copenhagen is beautiful," Lester said, lifting his glass of Caffè Royal as though shielding himself with it. "Beautiful and expensive."

Spencer set down his sandwich, took a cigarette with his free hand, put it in his mouth, lit it with a lighter that was shaped like a stethoscope, and, inhaling deeply, blew out a stream of smoke at his pal Lester. "Les, show Annie the pictures of the stainless-steel dinnerware you're getting for us," he said. "I want Annie to see the patterns."

As Lester fumbled in his pocket, Julius gave Annie a knowing look and rubbed his hands. "Getting the silverware, hey, Annie kid?"

"Show her the patterns," Spencer said to Lester, who produced brochures showing various designs of Danish stainless-steel flatware.

"They're going to get it in Copenhagen," Spencer said to Annie, "for three-fourths of what it costs at Georg Jensen's here."

"Twenty-five per cent off," Lester said joyously.

"Gee," Annie said.

"Show Annie the Obelisk," Spencer said. "Frankly, I like the Obelisk better than the Plata. Les and Julie like the Obelisk, too."

Annie tried to focus on the modern designs through her glasses. Obelisk or Plata—evidently that was what marriage meant to Spencer. Just the same, he was reaching for an emotion.

"Well," she said, "they're both very nice."

"Which is more you—the Obelisk or the Plata?" Spencer asked her. "Which do you choose?" He took another bite of his sandwich and then a quick puff on his cigarette.

"The Obelisk, hey, Annie kid?" Julius said.

"I don't care much for *any* silverware, really," she said. "I believe in using paper plates and paper forks and paper spoons and paper knives, and throwing them away after each meal. And paper cups, too. It's more efficient that way. I'm very lazy."

That sent Spencer and his friends into stitches.

"A riot, this kid," Julius said.

"The Obelisk," Spencer said, as though he and Annie had come to a decision. "Order the Obelisk, Les."

"Obelisk, hey, kids?" Julius said, bouncing up and down in his chair.

Annie decided to let it go, for the moment.

Lester wrote the order down. Then he and Julius finished their Caffè Royals and got up to go, saying they had some late shopping to do for their trip.

"I think I'll have a napoleon for dessert," Spencer said after they had gone. He stretched in his chair. She brought him the napoleon, and then attended to some nearby tables. When her stint was finished, Spencer offered to drive her home. She said yes. If she told Spencer she was going to the Zero Inn, he'd go with her, and trying to listen to jazz in his company was a strain. He was knowing about jazz, as he was about everything, and his enthusiastic comments had the peculiar effect of making all the fun and joy in the music funless and joyless. She would call Josh up when she got home.

"You ought to get away from these beatniks," Spencer said as she joined him outside. "These people are wrong for you. Frankly, I can't see why you work here."

"I like the people and they're not-beatniks," Annie said. "In fact, there's no such thing as a beatnik. What's more, I like the food, I like the atmosphere."

His car was parked across the street. "Frankly, I feel sorry for Julie," he said as they started off. "Julie says he doesn't want to be one of those Sunday fathers with Hugh. He'd rather not see Hugh at all. Just let Jean have him." He took her hand and squeezed it. "Frankly, Jean is in love with me," he said.

Annie woke up. "Gee, Spencer!" she said, delighted.

"Frankly, I loathe her," Spencer said. "The way she had me to dinner every night that time Julie had pneumonia."

"The dinner no good?" Annie asked.

"All right," Spencer said. "I was just being nice, keeping

her company while Julie ate in the bedroom. We did a lot of talking. About Hugh, and some intimate stuff about the physical difficulties she and Julie were having. Then, right after Julie got better, she calls me up and tells me she's got to see me. So I go over there, and she's alone. And she throws her arms around me and says she loves me and is going to divorce Julie."

"No kidding!"

Spencer sniffed. "I hate her," he said. "She's disgusting."

"What did you do?"

"I pushed her away!" Spencer said, reliving the moment of indignation with full force. "Two nights later, she called me up again and asked me to come over. What do you think she was doing?"

"Why did you go, Spencer?" Annie asked.

"She was alone again!" he said, ignoring Annie's question. "This time she was *crying*." He said it as if the crying were a major offense against him. "I hate her," he said, and added quickly, "Linda Beth is getting a custom-made dress from Balenciaga for the party. S. S. told me. S. S. is doing very well in his practice. Psychoanalysis has really opened him up. He's not as self-conscious, frankly, as he used to be about Linda's money. Of course, they're both in deep trouble, after four years. Both are in treatment now."

"Then maybe they won't have the party," Annie said.

But Spencer didn't hear her. "If we got married, it probably wouldn't last."

"If you get married and have ten years, that's a lot," Annie said. She thought of Josh. "And if you're lucky, it's more. And, besides, when you're really in love and have everything, it's so marvellous you don't think way ahead."

"Then let's get married," Spencer was saying.

"I don't mean us," she said. "I mean in general. I'm in love with somebody else. I *told* you."

"I don't care if it doesn't last," he said. "Nothing lasts anyway."

Annie had run out of replies. They drove slowly through crowded, narrow streets lined with tenements.

"This call will take a few minutes," he said, as though he had already told her that he had a call to make and she had been expecting all the time to make this stop on the way home.

He parked the car on a block of tenements that seemed to bear down heavily on tiny stores with cramped window displays of fish and shrimps, long Italian breads, sausage strings, straw baskets, handmade pottery, workmen's shoes. It was a warm night. The fire escapes were jammed with potted plants, dogs, blankets, pillows, cats, small children, and women in house dresses.

"I promised to be here two hours ago," Spencer said, taking his medical bag from the rear seat. He spoke in his usual manner of surprise at having forgotten that a patient was waiting for him somewhere. It always got Annie down to see how inured he was to the idea of sick people waiting. "I hope Elizabeth didn't give up and go to bed," he said. "I told you about her. With the spine. Remember?"

She remembered. The young woman who had developed a bone disease a dozen years ago. Annie couldn't remember the name of the disease, and she didn't ask. Elizabeth couldn't walk. She couldn't stand. She lived on home relief. She had a single relative—a brother, out in Colorado. She lived alone. Spencer had inherited her from an older doctor, who had got up a small fund that would take care of her medical expenses. The older doctor had retired to Florida after suffering a stroke. Annie wanted to wait for Spencer in the car, but he urged her to come in with him for a few minutes.

"There's nothing for me to do, frankly," he said. "I'll just look at her."

Fright clutched at Annie's insides. She was afraid of Spencer, afraid of Elizabeth. Why was he pushing this poor crippled girl at her? She followed Spencer into one of the tenement buildings, and down a narrow, dark, sour-smelling corridor, to a battered wooden door in the rear. There was no doorbell. He knocked, and, without waiting for an answer, tried the door. It was open. Brightness struck Annie full in the face—a small, crowded one-room apartment flooded with brightness. There was a narrow studio bed with a flowered chintz cover, and next to it a pink Princess telephone. There were bookshelves packed with paperbacks; a pastel-blue television set; a wall kitchenette, with a rectangle of wall the size of a pillowcase carefully papered with a design of carrots, lettuce, tomatoes, string beans, and onions. The bathroom door stood open to the room; the tub was rigged up with various mechanical contraptions. The girl, Elizabeth, sat in a wheelchair, her short blond hair neatly combed back straight off the forehead, her legs and back encased in aluminum, her face young, rosy, sweet, smiling, at peace in the classic expression of so many chronic invalids.

"Oh, Dr. Fifield!" she said. "I'm so happy to see you! I thought you weren't coming." No complaint. No resentment at his lateness.

"Annie Melvin," Spencer said, evidently assuming that an invalid's name was a dispensable part of an introduction.

The girl's hand when Annie shook it was warm and limp.

"Sit in my rocker," Elizabeth said to Annie. "It's my most comfortable chair. Would you like some coffee?"

"We just ate," Spencer said. His face was pale, vague, inert.

91

"You haven't been here for ever so long," Elizabeth said jubilantly. "You called that time and said you were coming, and you didn't come. See anything new around here?"

Spencer looked around sightlessly. "Didn't I call you back that time?" he said. "Something must have come up at the hospital. An emergency."

"Oh, I didn't mean that," Elizabeth said. "I just meant—Don't you see anything *new?*" She looked like a child about to spring a tremendous surprise. Unable to hold back any longer, she cried out, "My Princess telephone!"

"Mmmm, yes," Spencer said.

"It lights! Try it," Elizabeth said.

Spencer tried it. "Hmmm," he said. "It's the latest thing. A lot of my patients have it. Frankly, the Telephone Company is cleaning up with these."

Elizabeth's joy wasn't diminished in the slightest. "The relief investigator didn't like the idea much, because they say I'm not supposed to have luxuries. But this lights. I can see it in the dark. And anyway this was a present. From a friend."

"From that singer?" Spencer said.

"Gertrude. Yes," Elizabeth said, shyly and proudly. "And something else happened. Last Sunday, Gertrude called for me in a limousine, and we drove out to Bear Mountain for a picnic. It was the first time I'd been in the country since before winter. We had such a lovely picnic. Gertrude brought along this songwriter—Jeremy—and he roasted the frankfurters. They got burned." She looked over at Annie and laughed.

"Jeremy? Jeremy who?" Spencer asked.

"I don't remember, but he was awfully nice," Elizabeth said. "He's going to get up a whole new routine for Gertrude, so she can make her comeback."

"Frankly, I doubt that she can," Spencer said. "Gertrude's voice is gone. Frankly, she refuses to face it."

"But Gertrude says—"

"She's kidding herself," Spencer said, and sniffed.

"But Jeremy—"

"He's probably another one of these guys stringing her along," Spencer said. "Gertrude ought to wake up."

Annie saw a slight change in the girl's face, but very slight. She was still looking at Spencer with wonder. "I ate four frankfurters, Dr. Fifield. You would have been proud of me."

And Spencer smiled at her and said yes, he was very proud of her and she should get out in the country more often. Spencer looked really happy.

Annie stood up, and Spencer said, "I've got to get Annie home. We just came from one of the coffeehouses."

"The Freeplace," Annie said. "I'm a waitress there."

Spencer looked angry. "She's not really a waitress," he said to Elizabeth. "Annie's really a technician at the lab." He grabbed Annie at the back of the neck. Even in front of this girl! She started to free herself; then she saw Elizabeth smiling, happy to be in on the team act.

"How was the trip up to Bear Mountain?" Spencer asked Elizabeth, continuing to hang on to Annie. "Did you have any trouble with the ride?"

"Not a bit, Dr. Fifield!" Elizabeth said. "The limousine was perfect. They just rolled me up into it on one of those track things—you know?"

"Those track things are good," he said, and sniffed. "I've seen them work before."

"And I just rode in the chair in the car all the way up to Bear Mountain," Elizabeth said. "It was so easy."

"They have any trouble getting you out of the car up there?" he asked.

Elizabeth and Spencer were smiling at each other now, in perfect communication. It was as though Spencer suddenly could hear. What they were absorbed in was the mechanics of illness, but at the same time it was the mechanics of survival.

"You mean my legs?" she said.

"Yes."

"You won't believe this, Dr. Fifield, but first they pushed me in the wheelchair over the grass to the brick-grill place where the benches are—you know? And there was grass there, too. It looked so good I wanted to sit on it. And guess what?"

"You did!" Spencer said, looking very proud of his own correct guess.

"Just for a few minutes," Elizabeth said. "And I don't mind telling you, it felt darn good."

"Next time, get Gertrude to take you out to Jones Beach and try the sand," Spencer said.

"And those crowds!" Elizabeth said. They laughed, and Annie tried, with some effort, to join in.

"How's the contraption on the tub?" Spencer asked, letting go of Annie and moving to the bathroom.

"Well, I'm not exactly sure, Dr. Fifield," Elizabeth said. And again, together, they laughed.

Elizabeth started wheeling her chair after him, and Annie stopped her for a moment to say goodbye and tell them that she'd wait outside in the car.

About ten minutes later, Spencer came out of the building, tossed his medical bag into the rear seat, got in, and headed the car uptown.

"Elizabeth is in a bad way," he said, and sniffed. "Another

94

year or so, maybe sooner, and she probably won't be able to get around at all. . . . She depends on me. She looks forward to my visits. I should see her more often."

There was no indication in his tone that he intended to see Elizabeth more often. Still, when Annie looked at him he seemed thoroughly alive. For the first time since she had known him—alive.

"I'm glad you took me to visit her," Annie said. She was grateful for what she had seen between Spencer and this girl. In spite of everything that Spencer failed to do or tried to spoil for this girl, there was still something that he did, and something that Elizabeth did in return. And it was all Spencer had. In its own way, it was his love, his only love, and, Annie knew, he had tried to give it to her.

She had an urgent need to see Josh. To touch him. She wanted to ask Spencer to drive her back downtown, but she didn't. Instead, she silently said, "Thank you, dear Spencer, for the visit to Elizabeth. Thank you for dredging up out of your vacuum this fragmentary, true love."

★ VI ★

LATE ONE SATURDAY AFTERNOON, Annie left the Freeplace and found her brother in his car outside, waiting for her. It was a shabby, seven-year-old car, with egg-shaped holes in the hood, bent and rusting fenders, and an M.D. license plate. She looked at both car and brother with open affection and surprise.

"What do you know?" she said. "Mike's making the scene in the Village."

"O.K. Never mind the smart-aleck talk," he said, holding open the car door for her. He seemed pleased, in a rather abashed way, and yet clearly disapproving.

The lenses of her shell-rimmed eyeglasses were fogged with thumbprints. Her black hair was bunched wildly on top

of her head, and she was wearing her regular work costume—
black, flat-heeled slippers, no stockings, a cotton dirndl skirt
of multicolored stripes, and a black jersey turtleneck sleeve-
less top. Mike was flabby and round-shouldered, and his
face looked drained of rest and sleep. His eyes were like
his sister's, and he wore the same kind of glasses. He had on
a wrinkled navy-blue pin-striped suit that looked much too
heavy for the kind of warm Indian-summer day it was.

Annie gave a loud sigh and fell sidewise onto the front
seat, which was covered with a dark-gray terry-cloth towel
sagging with dampness and sand. With her toes she made
space on the floor for her feet, amid a litter of old medical
journals, a child's fading, cracked rubber ball, and a copy of
"Yertle the Turtle," the pages of which had been systemat-
ically ripped off in crescents at the corners.

"I had to make a house call around here," Mike said as he
headed uptown. "Thought I'd see if you wanted a lift home.
Got a date tonight?"

"No date."

He exaggerated his expression of disapproval and grunted.
Annie smiled and started singing a modern-jazz tune with
meaningless syllables made up of "b"s, "d"s, and "o"s. As
they drove, he occasionally glanced at her with an anxious
frown, but she stared straight ahead, singing, and they said
nothing to each other until they turned off the East River
Drive.

Seventy blocks to the north and some distance east of the
Freeplace, they came to a flashy new apartment house, its
glass-fronted lobby, one flight up and planted with fake
greenery, resting on top of a drugstore and a supermarket
overflowing with silvery shopping carts. Mike parked the car
near the drugstore and turned off the ignition. In the drug-

97

store, a tall, blond girl wearing heavy makeup and orange-colored toreador pants lounged backward against the soda counter, sipping an ice-cream soda. Under one arm she held a tiny monkey, who wore tiny orange-colored toreador pants and a matching orange-colored bonnet tied under his chin.

"Honestly, some of these good-for-nothing dames!" Mike said. He now directed his disapproval toward the girl in the drugstore, who surveyed the battered car and its occupant with amusement and contempt.

"That's-my-next-door-neigh-bor," Annie sang. "My-door-man-has-been-jiv-ing-a-round-with-her." She paused. "Or-the-oth-er-way-a-round."

"Annie!"

"Well, she's had two husbands already, and the doorman is always available," Annie said calmly.

"This smart-aleck way you talk," he said. "This crazy life you lead. Nobody to look out for you."

"Crazy?"

"You know what I mean. I don't want to put on a big-brother act, but who else is there but me? The kid brother Davy? A tennis bum living with that tennis-and-ski set of expatriates in Europe? One postcard from him in over a year! That's how much *he* cares!"

"He's very special," Annie said. "He's the only *glasses*-wearing tennis bum in history."

"Sure. And your sister Flora is very special, too. Another one who remembers us via Christmas card. Honestly, Annie, I worry about you. You don't have a regular life. Like normal people."

"I ought to move to the Village," Annie said.

"That's just what I mean," he said. "This crazy, irresponsible life you lead, hanging around with jazz bums, working in that coffee dump. As a waitress, for crying out loud. When you were trained in a profession. Honestly, I'm fed up with worrying about you coming home alone at crazy hours in the morning from that coffee dump. It's an irresponsible way to live."

"The Freeplace is not a dump!" Annie said. "It's a *caffè espresso,* and I love working there, if you must know. I just wish they'd put me on full time, instead of only four days a week. I love all those people who hang out there. They're the sweetest, gentlest souls on this earth."

"They're bums!" he said.

Annie gave a soft laugh. "I wish you'd visit the Freeplace," she said. "Where else can you get Capuccino coffee *and* Caffè Ghibellineo?" She picked up "Yertle the Turtle" from the floor and brushed sand from the pages.

"Joy won't go," Mike said, suddenly sounding weary. "Joy says it's all childish and immature. Listen, Annie, that's not the point anyway. The point is, you should go back to the hospital, where you belong, working with regular, normal people."

"With those death-pushers?" Annie put out her tongue and uttered sounds of revulsion. "Everybody at the lab gave me a pain. They made me feel bad."

"I don't understand it," said Mike. "Running away from a good job in the lab. Running away from Spencer Fifield, a nice, decent guy who wanted you to marry him and live like normal people."

"Spencer's all right, only he makes me feel terrible."

"He's a wonderful friend and a wonderful guy," Mike said. "And he's a damn good doctor."

"Except he wants everybody dead," Annie said. "As long as somebody is dead he's *for* them. All the dead Romans who

99

made it out. The dead Greeks. The dead Africans. The dead Jews. All the dead people he conducted into death as their doctor. Spencer loves *them*. He has a hard time 'relating,' as he puts it, to people who are alive, but, no doubt about it, he's a whiz with the dying. It's downright scary."

"Spencer is a good guy who wants to get married," Mike said. "He wants a home and a family."

"I got you, Pops," Annie said, and sighed.

"Anything, some little thing, that's not just right with Spencer will be fixed up in marriage," Mike said. "Believe me."

Annie shrugged. "All Spencer makes me feel is sorry for him. You know, when he asked me to marry him? He said to me, 'Frankly, I want a quiet wedding, with only our parents.' Parents! When he knew mine were *dead*. Besides, he's always grabbing me at the back of the neck. He thinks that shows people he's sexy."

"That's very important. My God, Annie! You want to become one of those dames in drugstores with a monkey? Look at her! Letting the monkey drink her soda!"

"I guess it's unsanitary," Annie said indifferently, watching the monkey lick at the glass.

Opening a straw handbag that was coming apart at the seams, she took out a cigarette and pushed in the lighter on the dashboard.

"It doesn't work," Mike said. "Honestly, Annie—"

"Why don't you get a new car, anyway?" Annie interrupted, her head practically inside her handbag. "What kind of doctor are you, anyway?" she asked, emerging with a book of paper matches. "Driving around in a wreck of a car with a lighter that doesn't even work? Don't you want to look successful to your patients? As though you get *paid*? What's the matter with you, man? You trying to make it as a saint?" She lit her cigarette and blew a neat, college girl's smoke ring at the windshield.

"Last night, when I got home, I had a long talk about you with Joy," he said, changing to a lighter tone. "I was bushed, too, believe me. A million house calls, then driving back to the beach. Joy says maybe that crazy jazz beatnik is giving you dope."

Annie let out a shrill yelp of pleasure, threw up her hands, and slid to the floor.

"I told her it was ridiculous," Mike said, looking nevertheless relieved. "Get up, Annie." His glasses were perspiring at the bottoms of the lenses. He took them off to wipe them, and, seeing how guileless and exposed his face was without them, Annie was touched. She slid back to the seat, removed her own glasses, and, with him, went through the motions of wiping off a layer of thumbprints.

"I don't mean that Joy knows anything," Mike said. "Her psychoanalyst tells her what to think. Last time I talked to him about her, he didn't seem to know who I was. He didn't even seem to know who *she* was. He sounded tired. They must get so tired they get all their patients mixed up with each other and with themselves."

Annie rolled down the window on her side and blew another neat smoke ring out toward the drugstore. "You know Stanley Stephen Klippenberg, at the lab?" she asked.

"S. S.?" Mike said. "Of course."

"You know he used to go to this lady analyst?"

"No kidding!"

"All day long at the lab, S. S. would come around talking about his lady analyst. Seems she had *her* couch all done up in ladylike chintz."

"No kidding!" Mike said again.

"S. S. would bend my ear about how his lady analyst was— the way he put it—'what I would call a real woman.' Did you ever hear anything so ridiculous? Endsville!"

Mike laughed.

"I couldn't stand it at the lab," Annie went on. "The way S. S. and Spencer latched on to stupid diagrams handed out by their head-feelers and pretended they were saying something, when all they did was talk."

Mike looked uneasy. "Joy asked Spencer to join us for dinner tonight at the beach, and we were hoping you'd come," he said quickly.

Annie said nothing.

Mike put on his glasses and pushed the nosepiece up with a forefinger. He cleared his throat and said, "We're taking Arnold and Thelma Lasher and the Pooleys to that new Chinese place, the Golden Eye. You remember Max Pooley, he took out Joy's appendix, and his wife, Irene." He continued talking fast. "You'd like the food at the Golden Eye, with all due respect to the Freeplace. It's real Mandarin cooking, not Cantonese. The real thing. It's sort of a dinner party. We owe both the Lashers and the Pooleys, and Joy is very fond of Spencer."

"We owe, you owe, they owe," Annie said. "It's so boring."

"It's the way regular people *live*," Mike said.

"What I mean is that Spencer is not *alive*," she said. "He's got his mind on trying to fit into a Brooks Brothers seersucker jacket. Or else he's got his mind on making up a grocery list of reasons why he likes me."

Mike held up his arms and flapped his hands at her with palms out. "All right, all right," he said. "All I asked was whether you wanted to join us for dinner tonight."

102

Annie was silent for a moment, and then she let out a deep breath. "I've got nothing better to do," she said. "Let's go."

"Don't you want to change?"

"Change? Why? Don't I look all right?"

"Well, sure," Mike said, starting the motor.

Annie waved goodbye to the monkey, and the blonde held the monkey's paw up and waved it back, thus causing the tiny toreador pants to fall to the monkey's feet. Mike laughed. He headed in the direction of Long Island. Little Andy had a cold, he explained, and Joy had arranged for everybody to meet at the Golden Eye, because she didn't want to create a lot of excitement in the house that might upset Andy and delay his recovery.

"Joy has these theories she makes up about recovery," Mike said plaintively. "I can't tell her anything any more. Her psychoanalyst is the only one she listens to. Her psychoanalyst has been telling her that she doesn't have self-esteem, and that she ought to buy herself more clothes, new clothes, to build up her self-esteem. So she lectures me about *my* lack of self-esteem. I still like to get my shirts and ties at Sears, Roebuck. Look at this tie!" One hand on the steering wheel, he used the other one to flip his necktie at her. "A real Paisley," he said proudly. "One buck."

"Terrifico!" Annie said.

Mike cautiously increased the speed of the old car and, watching for a safe opportunity, passed an open convertible packed with half a dozen teen-agers screaming the song "Jada."

"The good old days," he said. Then, with the parkway to Long Island open ahead, he said, "Lasher's trying to get us to move to Mount Vernon. He's been telling Joy how important it is to move in the right circles, make the right impression, be prepared to send Andy to the right camp. I don't get it."

"He's probably getting frantic up there all alone with Thelma," Annie said. "All Thelma ever wants to talk about is how she's 'working out,' in that crummy jargon, her marriage to Lasher. Thelma had this father who was very mean to her? And six years ago Thelma's psychoanalyst—she had a different one then—told her if she married Lasher, who was very unhappy at the time for his own reasons, she could do things for Lasher that she was never able to do for a father, and everything would get fixed up, or something like that. Anyway, for the past six years Thelma's been trying to find out how, for God's sake, everything got fixed up, because she says everything feels worse than ever, and she can't get over her mean father, and Lasher is still unhappy. So the new psychoanalyst is supposed to be helping her find out why. And that's all Thelma Lasher wants to talk about. Those jerky psychoanalysts. Those squares. They can hardly keep their own heads above water and they appoint themselves the final experts on other people."

"There must be some non-jerky ones," Mike said. "Only they're busy working, and you never hear about them. I'll bet Spencer has a non-jerky one."

"Blauberman. Al Blauberman."

"What did you say?"

"That's Spencer's analyst. This drag he goes to. This Dr. Al Blauberman of Scarsdale, U.S.A. Spencer used to tell me how terrible *Blauberman* felt. Isn't that too much? Blauberman complaining to Spencer on Spencer's twenty-five-dollar hours about getting snubbed by the high-*class* psychoanalysts? You know, the European ones who got a couple of letters from Freud thirty-five years ago and are still talking about it?

104

They're the élite. It seems that this drag Blauberman never made it with the élite psychoanalysts."

"How many of us will there be tonight who go to analysts?" Mike asked, and counted them off. "Joy. Thelma. Spencer. That gives the rest of us a majority. The Pooleys don't believe in psychiatry at all."

"He's a surgeon," Annie said. "He's got better ways of getting his kicks." She sighed. "You know, I miss the Freeplace? When I'm away from it, I really miss it."

Mike looked hurt.

"Sorry, Pops," Annie said, and stretched her legs. "How much farther?"

"About ten minutes." He retained his wounded air.

They were both silent, and then Annie said seriously, "It's just that you don't dig jazz musicians. All they try to do in music most of the time is make you feel good, you know? They make you swing. That means feel good. You know Vic Dickenson? He stands up there, blowing his trombone, and you can watch him trying to make you feel good. Even their *names* make you feel good. Chu Berry. Sweets Edison. Thelonious Monk. Pres."

"Pres?"

"Lester Young, president of saxophone players—that's why he was called Pres. He made it out last year. Spencer once did something terrible to Pres. We went to hear him, and Spencer asked him to play that awful song 'Love for Sale.' So Pres played it, making it sound wonderful, trying to make Spencer swing. Then Pres finished, and looked up expectantly at Spencer. Well, Spencer was yakking about Barnard or something and didn't even look at Pres. So Pres came over to him and said, 'You asked for that song, and then you didn't even give me a clap.'"

105

"Holy cow! Give us a rest!" Mike said, raising his voice. "Why do you have to make everything so complicated?"

Another few minutes of silence in the old car. Annie broke it. "Spencer is like some I.B.M. machine," she said. "He hears one word that connects with a mess of junk in his head and it releases everything he's got on the brain under that subject. He never swings." She received a sympathetic look from her brother, and went on, "Even when he asks you with words to make him swing, he never swings." She ran a hand through her dishevelled hair. "Spencer is always giving you a speech. He's got to be this big expert on everything. Say a name to Spencer. Any name. Kim Novak. Right away, he's got his mouth open to give you the real, inside, confidential dope on what's wrong with her and why."

"One thing you ought to learn is not to be so darn critical," said Mike.

"What I mean," said Annie, "it's all so discouraging, the way he tries to show he has some confidence. Spencer doesn't feel anything. He can't feel. When he wants to make a girl— or thinks he wants to, because his analyst tells him he should —you know what he says? He says, 'I need to be deeply involved with a woman.' He thinks all he's supposed to do is make this announcement."

"He's a nice, decent guy," said Mike. "Nice, decent guys don't know how to be smooth."

"Spencer blows cigarette smoke in my face," she said. "Don't you *see?*"

He let out a deep sigh.

"Once," Annie said, "when I was working at the hospital, I had a date to meet Spencer in the main waiting room. He was late. The only other person waiting there was an old man who was crying. In that high-pitched, muffled way. Then

106

Spencer showed up, looking happier than I'd ever seen him. So relaxed. Even his dimples were showing. He looked right through that old man. He cut right through the sound of the crying. And he launched into this big, loud, boorish speech about how he had just come from an emergency—a girl of twenty who had a brain tumor. They were going to operate that night. 'We just did the spinal tap on her,' he said. I swear he looked like a man who was fresh from a date with Elizabeth Taylor."

"He was only taking pride in his work."

"Spencer pretends to feel sorry for sick people," Annie went on, her voice shaking. "And to sympathize with people facing death. But he doesn't feel a thing. He uses their misery, because he wants them to love him. But he complains about patients who ask for real sympathy as though he's being persecuted."

"Well, my God! You can't feel real sympathy for everybody, or you'd go out of your mind."

"That's not what I mean. That's the way *you* are. You don't use medicine for something else."

"Well, there's the Golden Eye," said Mike.

"Nobody broke Spencer's arm and *made* him be a doctor," Annie said as Mike slowed the car.

"Annie, don't be a little sap," said Mike. "Spencer is a good guy. But nobody is forcing him on you."

The Golden Eye was a turquoise-and-chrome two-story modern palace modelled vaguely on a pagoda. At the door, Mike was hailed breezily by the Chinese maître d., a middle-aged, chubby, hard-faced man who seemed to combine all the attributes of his counterparts at Lindy's, "21," and the Chambord.

"Ah, Doctor, Doctor!" said the maître d. "Held up in some consultation, I presume, Doctor? This way, Doctor." All maître d.s love the sound of the word "doctor."

The rest of the party had already been seated at a round table for eight in a corner.

"How art thou?" Pooley shouted to Mike as chairs were reshuffled, hands shaken, napkins adjusted, smiles fixed. Pooley was a tall man with bushy white hair and a pince-nez, and he looked rather distinguished, when he wasn't talking.

"Oh, struggling along, Max, struggling along," Mike said.

"What took you so long?" Lasher asked. He resembled the Golden Eye's maître d. "You trying to make enough money to pay your income tax?"

Mike gave him a weak laugh.

"Mike never knows when to stop," Joy said, looking angry. "His patients don't appreciate it. He just gives and gives and gives." She was wearing a slim black dress and pearls —the suburban uniform of up-and-coming wives. She was a small, thin, pretty, prim girl with dark hair cut in Buster Brown style. She brushed cheeks with Annie.

"Hope I'm not contagious," Joy said in a high-pitched, nagging voice lifted with effort to sound like life-of-the-party. "Andy was coughing in my face all day long. Mike told him about covering his mouth. But Andy doesn't pay any attention to Mike. Mike doesn't get that proper tone of authority, or something."

Irene Pooley, a good-natured, big-boned woman in a large-flowered silk print dress, with fluffy hair as white as her husband's, giggled at Annie and, holding up a hand in a sort of Boy Scout oath, wiggled her fingers gaily at the latest arrivals. Then she turned back to Thelma Lasher, who was on the roly-poly side, like her husband, except that her face was narrow and drawn, and caked heavily with white powder. They were talking about salaries of schoolteachers in Mount Vernon versus those in Stamford, where the Pooleys lived, and whether teachers get psychoanalyzed on those salaries.

Spencer greeted Annie with enthusiasm. Grabbing her at the back of the neck, he managed to lower her to a place beside him. "Long time no see," he said, giving her costume a quick once-over, down to the slippers. "Capezios?" He raised his eyebrows knowingly. "How's the Freeplace?"

"Swinging," Annie said.

Spencer had on a brown-and-black striped raw-silk jacket, gray flannel slacks, and a proper tie. As soon as Annie saw him, she felt the old familiar sadness in her diaphragm. She turned to Lasher, on her other side. He patted her on the head. "How's my little beatnik?" he asked.

"Mike, the girls are dying for a drink," Joy said, with a playful smile. "Before you get lost in that nephrosis." He and Lasher and Pooley had quickly launched a medical discussion, talking across the wives.

"Be my guest," Pooley said to Joy, the fingers of one hand spread against his chest. He gave a guffaw.

Mike struggled to take intricate drink orders involving mixtures like pernod-vermouth-gin-with-lemon-peel and put them in the hands of the waiter.

"None of that mixed-drink malarkey for us, Sir Michael," Pooley said. "Make ours Scotch-and-soda, Chivas Regal."

Mike saluted with a forefinger at his temple. "Right, Max," he said.

"I need that drink," Irene Pooley said to Annie and the wives. "I saw my uncle today at the hospital. This old uncle of mine. He's got nobody but us. It made me feel dreadful."

"Can't"—Joy nodded at Max Pooley—"drop in to see him?"

"Mack the Knife?" Irene Pooley asked, in high humor. "Mack the Knife hardly has time to drop in on his own patients. This week he had a real run of gall bladders."

"They come in packs, like the Fifth Avenue buses," Lasher said. "Like ulceritis cases that used to jam up in the spring. Now I'm getting them all summer." Lasher was a gastrointestinal specialist.

"Ulcers don't recognize the seasons any more," Mike said. "Maybe it's because aggravation refuses to take a vacation."

"What I had thrown at me this week, I could *use* a vacation," Lasher said. He turned to Annie and patted her on the head again.

"The way you doctors eat," Annie said. "Funny *you* don't have trouble with your digestions."

"Little lady, the other doctors have me to protect them," Lasher said, and winked an eye at the table at large.

"I had trouble with me *teeth* last week," Pooley said, with indignation. "I went to see me old friend Itchy. He's a dentist. But we knew him when we were kids, so we still call him Itchy. We called him that because he was always scratching. Itchy is a hell of a dentist."

Spencer was quiet. Annie wondered why. Then she realized he was staring at a nearby table, where an aging, actressy-looking woman sat with a thin, delicate, jittery young man. Spencer squeezed Annie at the back of the neck, and said in an aside, confidentially, "Homosexuals love going out with older women. They can act out their hostility with older women. All homosexuals are basically unhappy people."

Pooley boomed out, "Itchy was frustrated because all he

110

found was one little cavity in me teeth. He filled it right then and there. With silver." He gave a hoot of pleasure.

"Mack the Knife got a little taste of his own medicine," said Mrs. Pooley.

"Poor Itchy!" Pooley shouted, demanding unified attention at the table, and getting it from most of the people in the restaurant. "Poor Itchy! He's forty-six and still single."

The maître d. skipped over to Mike. "Everything satisfactory, Doctor?"

"Tell him we want menus," Joy said to Mike.

Spencer stirred. "Frankly," he said, turning to Pooley, "all dentists I've ever known are neurotic. They're all frustrated doctors who lacked confidence to make the grade in medicine—which, frankly, most of the time was fully warranted." He nudged Annie to make her notice the table of the actress and her young friend. "Look, he's got one of those shoulder bags," he said.

Menus were handed around. The wives got to work studying them.

"I lose all inhibitions about eating when I come here," Joy said. "I'll be sor-ry."

"Mine host," Pooley said to Mike, "do we let ourselves go?" He took off his pince-nez and started to read the menu card from the top down.

"You think you have to be smart to be a doctor?" Lasher asked Spencer, with heavy, self-appreciative sarcasm. Having failed in two tries to make himself heard, he was asking it for the third time.

"Some doctors may be sharper than other doctors, but I'll take the less smart doctor any day," Mike put in. "I've seen too many so-called smart doctors go in for exploiting medicine. And I've seen a lot of doctors you might consider slow

111

or plodding, a lot of them working with the health-insurance organizations, who are really marvellous doctors. Why? Because they're faithful to medicine and have discipline. Who's for another drink?" he added quickly.

Lasher was stubborn about getting his point made. "You," he said, nodding his head at Spencer, "and I both know you neither have to be smart nor disciplined nor faithful to medicine to be *successful* as a doctor. Look at all these impostors. If they're not palming themselves off as F.B.I. men, they're doing surgical operations. Or those amateurs on submarines during the war who did appendectomies with a spoon. Of course, surgery is easy. Surgery is one thing, medicine is another. But I know plenty of dentists who would make terrific surgeons or internists."

"Easy!" Pooley shouted. "It's easy only if you're not a surgeon. And let me tell you, you need brains to know how to use a knife. I'm tired of being called dumb."

"Did I call him dumb?" Lasher asked Spencer.

But Spencer was not listening. He looked directly at Lasher, as though he were talking to him, but he said, "Frankly, I just realized the other day what a good doctor S. S. Klippenberg is. He's really a good doctor. He really wants his patients to get well."

"For crying out loud, what kind of doctor *doesn't* want his patients to get well?" Annie asked.

"Mike, the girls want to order," Joy said.

The menu of the Golden Eye was decorated with fat green dragons and fat gold Buddhas. On each Buddha's stomach was a Chinese inscription with a translation in parentheses, such as "One of our dinners is more precious than rubies and diamonds" or "Our customers leave this place with a broad smile."

112

"Frankly," Spencer said, as everybody bent over a menu, "the best dish in the house is Heng-yen Chi-ding."

"Everything here is delicious," Mike said. "It's real Mandarin cooking."

"What the hell is Heng what?" Pooley yelled across the table to Spencer.

"Chicken with almonds," Spencer said. "But different from anything you ever had."

"How would you know?" Lasher asked sarcastically.

It took quite a while to record the orders of Curry Niu, Lobster Soong, and so on. Thelma Lasher said she wanted only Wonton soup, and it took at least ten minutes for the others to persuade her to eat something. The more they shoved food and sympathy at her, the more she resisted. Wonton soup only it remained, until Pooley, who had ordered Heng-yen Chi-ding, changed his mind.

"The hell with it," he said. "Make mine chicken chow mein. That's what I always go for at the Chink's."

"Not me," said Irene Pooley, "I love all these exotic dishes. But it makes me feel guilty to eat all these things when some people in this world are going hungry. I go absolutely crazy when I go to Trader Vic's. Those cocktail Kau Kau! Their Cho-Cho! And Po-Po!"

"Guilt," Thelma Lasher said. "What do you know about guilt?" Then she, too, said she would have some chicken chow mein. It developed that the Mandarin menu did not include chicken chow mein. So the maître d. was called over for help in the emergency.

"Certainly, Doctor," the maître d. said to Mike, making a thumb-and-forefinger circle high in the air. "We'll dish it up somehow, Doctor."

"That's the girl!" Pooley said, beaming at Thelma Lasher. "When in Rome, do as old Professor Pooley does."

Irene Pooley said, "Oh, I don't know, Thelma. I believe we have our share of guilt in Stamford, too."

Mike sent Joy a message with his eyebrows to start a Stop Thelma Lasher movement.

"I just love Stamford," Joy said hastily. "I love those white wooden houses—Colonial, aren't they? Those green, rolling lawns. The country is a wonderful atmosphere for rearing children."

"You ought to move to Mount Vernon," Lasher said. "To your health." He raised a freshly served drink and took a large gulp.

Annie sipped her drink and said, "I saw a sign on the Merritt Parkway last week. It said, 'Don't put your elbow out too far / Or it may go home in another car.' The only piece of poetry between New York and Stamford, and it has to be that."

"It's getting worse and worse in the suburbs all the time," Spencer said, lighting a cigarette. A match spark dropped on Annie's skirt. Jumping abruptly to his feet, he brushed Annie off, drew deeply on the cigarette, and exhaled heavily at the nearby faces. "I've had four new patients this week, all of them suburban housewives," he went on, and sat down again. "All of them unhappy. All of them with symptoms of G.I. disorders. They get bored. They have nothing to do. They're full of hostility toward their children and toward their husbands. Suburban women are the worst women I've ever met in my life," he said with relish. "Grasping, selfish, empty, materialistic, useless. The worst."

Irene Pooley gagged on her drink. "Well—" she gasped as Lasher, on the alert, pounded her on the back. She had to hold off his hand to stop him. "Well, I wouldn't generalize, Spencer," she said, finally. "I'm a woman. I'm living in the suburbs. And *I* don't hate my husband and children."

Spencer gave no sign of having heard her. "A lot of them are playing around with other men," he went on.

Appetizers were placed on the table. Spencer helped himself to a large fried shrimp, popped it into his mouth, and chewed on it with zest. "With milkmen. With mailmen. With truck drivers. With gardeners. With golf pros. And a lot of them go in for homosexuals."

"Twenty-three skiddoo!" Pooley said. "Oh, you kid!"

"How about sending some of those women over to my office?" Lasher asked. "If, as you say, they have the symptoms you say."

Thelma Lasher gave her husband a sad look.

"On the other hand, skip it," Lasher said. "You're better at handling these screwballs anyway."

"Frankly, these women don't have a thing wrong with them," Spencer said. "Physically speaking."

"I get together with a bunch of the girls every other Wednesday, and we read the Great Books," Irene Pooley said. "We meet at each other's houses. Would you call that bored?"

"Pussycat, Spencer is needling you," Pooley said.

Spencer helped himself to another shrimp, and puffed at his cigarette at the same time. He finished his drink. Then he went on. "A lot of these horrible suburban women have waited years, frankly, to get even with their husbands," he said.

Irene Pooley looked as though she might cry. "I even got Mack the Knife started on reading—didn't I, hon?" she said to her husband. "We read Dickens out loud every night. We've gone all through Dickens, and now we're starting all over again."

"I'm hot for Dickens," Pooley said, and laughed. "I got aholt of meself last year and gave meself a good talking to," he went on. "I said to meself, 'Look here, boy, you spend half a day cutting and half a day looking at what you did cut or what you're going to cut. Relax.' And Pussycat came along with Dickens and saved me."

The main course arrived and put an end to the discussion.

Pooley rubbed his hands exuberantly over his chow mein before getting to work on it. "This is what I call eating Chink's," he said to Mike. "I may eat you out of house and hearth. Hope you brought along enough in the way of *argent?*"

Mike held up a traffic-stopping palm, and everybody settled down in a fairly concentrated way to the meal.

Annie loved snow peas. She was very grateful when Spencer slipped a couple of snow peas from his plate onto hers. But naturally he had to go and spoil things. "Isn't this better than the Freeplace?" he asked. "Frankly, Dr. Blauberman can't understand why you stick with those beatniks."

"Beatniks?" Annie asked, her voice beginning to quaver. "What exactly do you mean by beatniks?"

By now, the group was coming up from plates for air. Lasher reached over and patted Annie on the head again. "Don't mind Spencer," he said. "I'm with you, sweetie-pie. So long as you keep me away from the weirdos with the beards, the ones that don't ever take a bath."

"The weirdos with the beardos?" asked Pooley.

"I heard a terrible story about a beatnik from my analyst," Thelma Lasher said. "We were talking about the way my sister died. The baby. She choked on something, and I always felt it was my fault. My analyst told me about a beatnik who had a baby and then refused to take care of it. Just let the baby sit in a corner while she continued on with all her beatnik ways."

116

"How's the baby now?" Annie asked. Nobody answered her.

Joy said, "There's something deeply disturbed about a mother who will abandon her own child."

"To understand that you need analysis?" Lasher asked.

"That baby doesn't sound abandoned," Annie said. "Obviously, that mother let the baby sit in a corner and watch everything. Babies love to watch everything that goes on. That mother sounds smart to me—including the baby in."

Joy gave her a what-do-you-know-about-motherhood look. "I wouldn't trust any beatnik with my child," she said. "They aren't normal."

"My analyst said the way the baby was treated was worse than the way they didn't watch my sister," Thelma Lasher said bleakly.

"I'm glad he tells you something," Lasher said. "For my twenty-five hard-earned bucks an hour."

"Beatniks? What are all these beatniks?" Pooley asked.

"A bunch of well-intentioned kids—nice kids, basically," Mike answered. "They just don't work. They're bums. They have a lot of energy left over, because they don't get up at seven every morning, like we do, to go to work. A beatnik puts on the old T shirt and he's all dressed."

"They're not nice kids at all," Spencer said, with his customary authority. "They're nasty and dishonest. Take my last secretary. She used to steal drugs from me. One day she stayed home with a cold, and I dropped in on her without warning. I found her in bed with a dope addict."

"Why did you drop in unannounced?" Irene Pooley asked.

Spencer ignored her. "You can't trust any of them," he said. "They lie and steal and cheat, and they sleep with anybody." He sounded oddly hysterical, and went on relent-

117

lessly, "I caught her in the act. I confronted her with what she is. I told her off but good. Frankly, these beatniks are nothing but little tramps."

Annie had opened a fortune cookie. "This is for you, Spencer," she said, and read, " 'Better be an old man's sweetheart than a young man's slave.' "

Fruit was served, flaming in fired brandy. The maître d. came over to check up on it. "Everything all right, Doctor?" he asked, bowing to Mike. He made three additional bows and retired.

Annie was getting a stomach-ache. "I could use an *espresso*," she said to Spencer. But he was busy with his own thoughts, and with his own fortune cookie. " 'A real friend is one who will tell you of your faults,' " he read.

"That's meant for an analyst," Thelma Lasher said.

"Frankly, I don't agree with it," said Spencer, crumpling up the sliver of paper and throwing it on the floor.

"Why, pray tell?" asked Pooley, who never minded being a straight man.

"Because, frankly, it's not appreciated," said Spencer. "I tried it once. On ward service. With that girl who's been on the ward for months, with colitis. She used to keep washing her hands every five or six minutes. Her hands were raw. Sore. All the skin gone. One day, I decided to experiment. So I threw a guess at her about what was causing her disturbance. She looked at me like a wild animal, and flew at me, clawing with her fingernails. I had set off a psychotic episode. I had hit on the truth." He pursed his lips in a caricature pose of doctor-in-deep-thought.

Annie had heard Spencer tell this story several times. It was one of his old favorites.

"You don't kid around with a colitis," Lasher was saying.

118

"These colitis people suffer miserably," Mike added. "I always try to give them a little extra t.l.c."

"She's such a pretty kid, too," Spencer said. "It's too bad. And she's going to be in for more trouble, too. You know that nurse on the ward? Baker?"

"The blonde?" Pooley said. "Who doesn't?"

"She's a tramp; all she thinks about is sex and having a good time," Spencer said. "But I've got something on her that's going to get her thrown out of the hospital. Too bad the colitis girl is so attached to her."

"Baker is wonderful with that kid," Lasher said. "Baker has been able to get her to eat. Which is more than the doctors could do. Baker is a marvellous nurse."

"What do you mean, a tramp?" Mike asked. "Is Baker a beatnik, too?"

"Worse," Spencer said. "I found out she helped perform an abortion on one of the ward cases."

"In the hospital?" Pooley asked in amazement.

"Outside," said Spencer. "Somewhere in Brooklyn. This Negro woman was on the ward with a minor pneumonia and started telling Baker all her troubles. Seven other kids. No money. No husband in the house. One kid crippled by polio. The usual story." Spencer sniffed.

Everybody was quiet, waiting for him to go on. He sniffed again, lit a cigarette, and said, "She begged Baker to get her an abortion. And Baker did it."

"How do you know about it?" asked Annie.

"She told me herself."

"The Negro woman?" Joy asked.

"No. Baker herself."

"When did she tell you?" Mike asked. "How come?"

"Oh, we had a few drinks one night and got to talking.

You know how it goes. I'm going to get her thrown out of the hospital. She's a no-good tramp."

Lasher reached for the glass still holding a quarter inch of his last drink and swallowed the remains. "With the shortage of nurses, Spencer, you can't go around investigating their morals. We're interested in their nursing. Baker does wonders with the patients. With that colitis."

"Too bad," Spencer said, trying to put a sorry look on his face. "The poor kid was so attached to Baker."

Annie drew a deep breath. "Why don't you mind your own business, Spencer? Why don't you leave that nurse alone?" Her face was so warm the lenses of her glasses became cloudy, and she saw Spencer as a kind of formless shape.

"It has nothing to do with her," he said. "It's my duty to the hospital. We can't let her get away with it. It gives the hospital a bad name."

"We could go to Baker and ask her not to do it any more," Mike said. "She's very warmhearted. She means well."

"Why, she was only trying to help that poor woman," Irene Pooley said.

"Knock it off, Spencer," said Pooley, completely un-clowned. He sounded disgusted. "What are you after the poor dame for?"

"You out of your mind?" Lasher asked Spencer. "We need good nurses."

Joy took Spencer's arm and twined hers around it. "Don't be silly, Arnold," she said to Lasher. "Spencer is only trying to help the hospital. You don't have to do it that way, Spencer. Do it the way"—she nodded at Mike—"he says."

Even Thelma Lasher spoke up for Baker. "Sometimes it's better not to have the baby at all than to have one that doesn't have a chance in life."

120

Mike sighed and signalled to the maître d. to bring the check, as though that settled the Baker matter. "We'll talk to Baker this weekend," he said. "Invite her out to dinner or something."

"No!" Spencer said. He pulled away from Joy and looked at the others. His eyes were shining. "I've already reported her to the nurses' supervisor."

There was a terrible silence. Spencer was calm and smiling as he faced their combined rage.

Mike turned to Annie, as if to say that now he understood. But Annie, mourning for Spencer, had reached over and lightly placed her hand on his sleeve.

★ VII ★

AT THE BEACH, it was raining almost noiselessly, with gray lumps of wetness hanging over the sand dunes and the houses behind them. In the living room of the 1928-ish gabled, clapboard year-round house at the beach front, a small fire in the brick fireplace gave out no heat and slowly died as father and child sat on the sofa together in disharmony. Andy, at five, could be troublesome if he wanted to, and, sitting—or, rather, spread out in dissatisfaction—on Mike's lap, he wanted to. Mike had some difficulty holding the book in his hand as the boy, whining, squirmed. A neighbor's child, also five, stood in front of them, his buck-toothed face three inches from Mike's, noticing everything.

"The name of this book is 'One Fish, Two Fish, Red Fish,

122

Blue Fish,'" Mike said. Hugging the boy on his lap with his elbows, pointing over him with his chin, in encouragement, to the appropriately colored words on the title page, he said, "Now you read it, Andy."

Before Andy could open his mouth, the buck-toothed wonder from the house across the street put in breathlessly, "One fish two fish red fish blue fish I know the one fish book I learned it all Dr. Melvin. I learned the whole book I know it."

"Very good, Guy," Mike said evenly, surprised at the power of the sudden rage within himself at this interference.

Guy's legs gradually slid away from each other in a split. His sun-bleached yellow mop of hair was uncut and uncombed. He was wearing light-blue cotton shorts with an elastic top, and they were several sizes too large for him. The Indian on horseback embossed at the hemline came below the little boy's kneecap. The shorts were all he was wearing against the cold, damp autumn day. He smelled of sea salt and ice cream.

"Come on, fella," Mike said to Andy, edging back on the sofa, away from the blunt, untroubled stare of the visitor. "Don't you want to read the fish book?"

Mike felt the sullenness in the child on his lap, felt it matching his own. He was pinned down in the house on this rain-soaked day while Joy marched off to the city to see the damn psychoanalyst. There would be no relief for hours. She wouldn't get back until after six. From the psychoanalyst, she was going shopping for new clothes, she had announced. What on earth was there about psychoanalysis that sent wives steaming away straight from the couch into Bergdorf Goodman? All those little directives on how to buy clothes, no doubt, as well as on how to eat, how to talk, how to think, how to be popular, how to make love. The latest directive was

123

that Mike should spend at least one afternoon a week in the house taking care of Andy. So, to please Joy's psychoanalyst, he had been forced to readjust his office hours and reschedule visits to patients in and out of the hospital who had serious physical illnesses that were a damn sight more important than anything that was the matter with Joy. And for what? Joy was becoming impossible. She kept throwing meaningless pseudo-psychiatric jargon around and didn't have the faintest understanding of what it meant. Everything she didn't like at the moment or couldn't comprehend, about Mike or anybody else, was labelled "not normal." And, by some coincidence, Andy now spent over half his life whining about everything, normal or not normal.

"Guy, don't you want to sit down?" Mike asked, trying to disguise his impatience.

"Uh-uh." Guy moved in half an inch closer.

In the kitchen, which was next to the living room, the washer-dryer, set going by Joy before she took off, shifted gears loudly; the clanking wheeze became a nerve-racking buzz as the machine got ready to toss the clothes around inside. There was an equally violent commotion on Mike's lap. Andy had pulled off his white sandals and white socks, and was simultaneously struggling to rip off his white T shirt and kicking at Guy.

Mike stopped him, replaced the white socks and white sandals, and held down the T shirt. "Come on, now, fella, you'll catch cold," he said, aware of the ingratiating, placating, babying tone in his voice. Andy started to kick and cry again.

"He's upset Dr. Melvin because he pushed over the monkey-sticks bridge you built before and now he's sorry he did it," Guy volunteered.

Before the reading session, Mike had spent a half hour building Andy and Guy a four-level bridge with sharp-pointed plastic sticks—an unworthy substitute for the Erector set that had been the delight of his own boyhood. The moment it was completed, Andy had struck it down. He had been crying and whining since. The afternoon had got off to a beaut of a start.

"He won't catch cold, Dr. Melvin," Guy said. "Look at me I never wear shoes unless we go to Manhattan. We may go to Manhattan tomorrow and then I'll wear shoes."

"Life is simple for some people," Mike said, secure in the knowledge that only a couple of five-year-olds heard him.

"Feel me I'm hot," said Guy, eagerly taking Mike's free fist and kneading it.

Sure enough, the visitor's little brown hand pulsed with fire and energy. Mike became aware of the cool clamminess of his own hand.

Andy dived off his lap and made for the telephone, near the steep, zigzag, linoleum-covered stairway leading up to the bedrooms. He picked up the receiver, dialled a few digits, and said into the telephone, "Tell her to call me up right away because I have to do something. I don't know what I have to do but I have to do it." He hung up and, apparently feeling better, returned to his father's lap. In passing Guy, he stepped craftily on Guy's foot.

"Ow!" said Guy.

"Now you read, Andy," Mike said, snubbing the guest's protest.

"I hate this *book*," Andy said.

"One fish, two fish—" Mike began.

"Stupid fish, foo-foo fish," Andy said. He looked up in pleased amazement as Guy echoed shrilly, "Foo-foo fish!"

Guy then lay, belly down, on the floor, in a breast-stroke position. "Foo-foo fish!" he shrieked. Andy slid down to the floor and imitated him. In the background, the duomatic washing machine whistled three times and moved ahead into dry cycle or delayed bleach or some goddam-fool thing.

"Blinkyfish! Stinkyfish! Stunkyfish!" Guy yelled, leaping up. He headed for the stairway. Andy followed him. From upstairs, the pounding of five-year-old feet thudded at Mike's temples, and his head began to ache. Then the herd crashed down the linoleum-covered stairs and returned, screaming, to the living room.

"Tell you what, fellas!" Mike shouted above the din as Guy led an obstacle race over the furniture and climbed up on the teak-topped Georg Jensen coffee table. Andy climbed up after him and started kicking a few fresh dents into the table, which dated back nine years to wedding-present days.

"Get off that table! Off! Off the table!" The proper note, for a change, was sounded. The boys wilted, momentarily.

"Fellas—now, everybody," Mike said. "How about some movies? I can get out the movie machine."

"Donald Duck!" Guy yelled, panting.

Andy picked up a butterfly net and brought it down over Guy's head. "I hate stinky Donald Duck," he said, and Guy said, "Dammit get this butterfly net off my head!"

His parents believed in freedom of speech for everybody, including children. Maybe that was the way to do things. But Joy had made a big complaining point about how such lack of discipline produces insecurity, free speech to Joy being synonymous with lack of discipline. So Mike, feeling bored and tired, and hearing the washing machine clatter with finality and subside, made a stab at pleasing his absent wife. "Take it easy, fella," he said to Guy. "You don't have

126

to use naughty words." Naughty. He hated that word. But it was one of Joy's words, and he went along with it.

"'Dammit' is O.K., Dr. Melvin. My mother said 'dammit' is O.K."

"We don't use naughty words in this house."

Guy stared him down. "My mother said not to pay attention if people tell me something is naughty, she said 'naughty' doesn't mean anything."

"Dammit!" Andy yelled. "Dammit dammit! I hate Donald Duck!" He nabbed Guy again with the butterfly net.

Guy pulled the net off his head and, letting go abruptly, caused Andy to fall back on the hard linoleum.

More crying. Wailing.

"Shut up!" Mike shouted. "Maybe I'll show 'Ben-Hur.' Clark Gable and Charles Laughton in 'Mutiny on the Bounty,' maybe. Orson Welles in 'Citizen Kane'! 'Hell's Angels,' with Jean Harlow! 'Gone with the Wind'!"

The distraction worked. Mike continued shouting like a maniac, and the boys giggled at him in united admiration.

" 'Destry Rides Again'! 'The Asphalt Jungle'! 'Children of Paradise'! 'Bride of Frankenstein'! 'À Nous la Liberté'! 'Potemkin'! 'Ten Days That Shook the World.' 'The Sea Wolf.' I'm going to show movies," Mike went on in a calmer tone. "I'm going to show 'The Big Parade,' maybe, and maybe not, maybe 'Little Women,' and maybe not, maybe 'The Cabinet of Dr. Caligari,' maybe not . . ." He continued talking thoughtfully, hypnotically, and led his charges over to the front closet, where he rummaged around on the shelf for the movie projector, the portable screen, and the boxes in which he kept all the home movies he had made since he was in college. For the past five years, almost all the movies had starred Andy.

"And if I can't find Jean Harlow or 'The Cabinet of Dr.

Caligari,' I'll show movies of Andy as a little baby," Mike went on, sensing, for the first time that afternoon, that peace was at hand; the boys were with him. They stood behind him respectfully as he took all the equipment and movie files down from the closet shelf. They tried to help him as he put up the white screen at one end of the room, closed the window blinds, placed the projector in position, and haphazardly opened the boxes containing reels of film.

"Now, let's see," Mike continued. " 'Ben-Hur,' 'Ben-Hur,' or shall we have a little Jean Harlow, maybe, or Greta Garbo or Carole Lombard—hey, fellas?"

He pawed over reels labelled "HOSPITAL—GOING HOME—JULY 1956" and "BATH—SUMMER 1956" and "XMAS 1959" and "BIRTHDAY PARTY—FOURTH—7/10/60."

"Daddy, will you show the movie of the little tiny baby getting his hair washed and Mommy is holding him?" Andy asked, changed into a new boy—obliging, sweet, rational, eager, filial, coöperative.

"Lights, Andy!" Mike commanded. His son jumped to obey, turning on the light, awaiting further orders. A pleasure. Mike fitted a reel into position and got ready to roll.

"Lights out!" Mike said. Again, Andy, knowing what was expected of him, did what Mike wanted, and then ran to his place on the sofa, facing the screen.

MERRY CHRISTMAS 1959

The boys watched, bouncing up and down with enjoyment, as the color movie showed a red-ribboned sparkling green paper wrapping being torn off a box by out-of-focus hands.

Andy called the scenes out in advance, knowing the shots

by heart. "Andy's first suit!" he announced, standing up, as a collarless, lapel-less navy-blue jacket with short pants was handed over in anonymous hands to Mike on the screen. "Daddy tickles the suit!" On the screen, Mike obeyed, taking the suit, turning it face up, and indeed tickling a middle jacket button.

The other member of the audience hummed in enthusiastic appreciation. All was still well.

Another reel was started.

SUMMER 1956

Reverent silence in the audience as Joy came on the screen, wearing a housecoat, holding an eyes-closed, head-teetering weeks-old baby on her shoulder.

"Andy! Andy! It's Andy!" Andy exclaimed.

Joy held the baby to her cheek. She held the baby aloft. She put the baby on her lap. Closeup of the baby sleeping in his crib. Closeup of Daddy—a slimmer, glazed-eyed Daddy —his finger held in the baby's fist. Closeup of Joy, a rather puzzled-looking Joy, pretty, stiff, wary, her Buster Brown hair style impeccably in place, looking down at the baby in his crib. Then the camera came closer to the crib, closer and closer to the baby, blank-faced and blurred, and the reel was finished.

"Lights!" Mike shouted.

Guy usurped the privilege, turning on the light. Andy did not object.

"Daddy, you didn't show where the little tiny baby is getting his hair washed."

"Well, we'll see about that," Mike said. "We'll show that one a little later, if we can." He rewound the film and then,

129

fumbling with another reel, fitted it into the projector. "Now, let's see what we have here. Lights out! . . . Well, what do you know?" Mike said, in mock surprise. "This movie is of Daddy in the old days, when Daddy went to school."

No opposition from the audience. On the screen, the beautiful, beautiful green hills; the town in the foothills, where he had roomed with Mrs. Kelly, who had taken six dollars a week and left him alone; where Geraldine had a ground-floor apartment complete with icebox and stove, with the oversized studio bed that could hold nine people sitting upright at parties, and with the fireplace, the portable record-player, and the stacks of books and magazines on the floor. A shot of the rooming house, gray and wooden, not unlike his present home. The back-door entrance to Geraldine's room. Oh, my God! The warmth in that room! Even in upstate winters, with the snow piled ten feet high outside and the temperature down to six below, it was always warm in that room. On terribly cold nights, Geraldine would light the oven and heat up her nightgown, along with his pajamas, like bread. And they would get into bed warm.

"Where is the school, Daddy? I don't see the school."

Mike could feel his heart palpitating. His head throbbed. He took off his glasses and put them aside. He could not look away from the screen to the boy. Nearsighted as he was, he could clearly see the image on the screen without his glasses. He could see every small detail of the old house. The white-and-red French curtain on the windowed door to Geraldine's room. "This is a different kind of school. It's where Daddy went to medical school, where he learned how to make sick people get all better," he said mechanically. He was in that room. He could feel it. He could smell it. Oven-baked pajamas.

Tennis courts on the screen. Geraldine playing tennis with

130

him on the courts behind the Social Science Building. Peggy or Eric must have taken the movies of him. Probably Eric, with that particular shot of the beautiful courts—beautiful red clay, always rolled, shaded by elms and weeping willows, sunk in a hideout between hills. "The most beautiful campus in the world," all the alumni said to each other, and it was true.

Peace. Peace and tennis. A quick shot of him running for the ball deep in a corner of the court, retrieving the ball, returning it, running for the answer in the opposite corner. The old days. He had never given up. He had always run for them, even when it had looked hopeless.

Restive rumblings in the audience. He started talking fast again. It was possible for him to keep on talking, as long as he could keep his eyes on the screen. "There's Daddy playing tennis. See Daddy? See Daddy's eyeshade?"

"Daddy?"

"Sure, it's Daddy, sixteen, seventeen years ago. Daddy wore an eyeshade because it's so clear up there in the hills you can see a firefly at night ten miles away. There's nothing between you and the sun."

"I hate fireflies," Andy said. "They're beetles."

"Dr. Melvin, is that lady Mrs. Melvin?" Guy asked.

"No, that's Geraldine." Mike rubbed the palms of his hands against his trousers.

"Geraldine?" Guy said.

"Geraldine?" Andy said.

"Geraldine went to medical school with Daddy. And now she's a doctor, too, and she makes people well, and here she's playing tennis with Daddy and making him run for the hard ones. There was always time in those days to play tennis and everything. The old days."

On the screen, the scene had shifted. Closeup of Geraldine,

sitting on the grass with two other girls, also in tennis clothes. Geraldine smiled at the camera and waved, good-natured, relaxed, somewhat on the heavy side, awkward, full-bosomed, and soft-faced. The boys laughed at Geraldine on the screen as she did an imitation of her clumsy self reaching for a tennis stroke and muffing it. The other girls on the screen were laughing. Nice girls. Generous. Warm. God, the warmth!

Now they were back in Mrs. Kelly's yard, having a picnic. They had spent whole days and nights in that yard, eating, talking, studying, and sleeping away the hot September nights. The yard had an outdoor grill. A shot of frankfurters broiling on the grill. Strictly an Eric-type shot.

"Yikes, hot dogs!" Andy screamed.

"I ate four hot dogs yesterday, Dr. Melvin," Guy said. "My father fixed a cookout."

"Very good, Guy," Mike said, studying the screen.

"I ate six seven nine hot dogs!" Andy said. "Stinky hot dogs!"

"Stinky-winky hot dogs!" Guy said. "Stinky hot dogs!"

"Stinky hot dogs," said Andy.

The boys rocked with forced laughter. Mike hardly heard them.

"Dammit hot dogs dammit!" Andy screamed at his father.

"He said 'dammit,' Dr. Melvin," Guy reported obligingly.

No recognition.

Winter. The trees, the yard, the roads heavy with mounds and angles of snow. In front of a high snowbank, Geraldine grinning at him under two woollen scarves wrapped around her head. Her brown, badly fitting coat blowing in the wind. Her boots as clumsy as a Russian peasant's. She provided action for the camera. She took off enormous green woollen mittens, blew on her hands, held the hands up stiffly, as though frozen, to the eye of the camera. Mike could taste the snow-wet woollen mittens in his mouth.

"Once I made a snowman, Dr. Melvin," Guy said.

"Dad-dy," Andy said, whining again. "I want the little tiny baby getting his hair washed." He started taking off his sandals. Mike didn't notice him.

FINALS

The title was crudely lettered.

" 'Finals,' " Mike read to the boys. "Pay close attention, now, everybody."

On the screen, Geraldine, Peggy, and Mike were studying, seated at a card table set up in the yard. Good old Eric, on the job again. Geraldine obliged the camera by hitting herself on the head and putting on an expression of pain and dismay.

Guy laughed at Geraldine's antics.

"Who's that lady, Dr. Melvin?"

"I told you. Geraldine."

"Is Geraldine Andy's mommy?"

"No."

"Is the other lady?"

"No."

"What's she *doing* now?" Guy asked. "Why is she closing her eyes? She looks funny."

"She's studying. She's memorizing. That's the way Geraldine studies." Mike felt himself smiling.

"Where's Andy?" Andy whimpered. "Where's Mommy?"

"Well, Mommy and Andy weren't with Daddy in medical school," Mike said dully, indifferent to the boy, indifferent to the guest, indifferent to the beach.

133

The screen blanked white. The celluloid film slapped against the machine.

Andy jumped up quickly and put on the light. He was barefoot. In the dark, he had undressed himself so that he, too, wore only shorts. "Now show movies where the little tiny baby is getting his hair washed?" he asked.

Mike blinked at him in the light. He neither saw the boy nor heard him. He was alone in a cold room.

* VIII *

IN DR. BLAUBERMAN's OFFICE, on the seventeenth floor of a
new Fifth Avenue apartment house facing Central Park,
Ephraim Samuels was lying on the analytic couch, saying
nothing. Dr. Blauberman sat near the head of the couch,
where Ephraim could not see him, in a gigantic chair that
tilted up at the feet and down at the back, to rest his heart
and improve his general well-being. The chair was uphol-
stered in cream-colored leather, and Dr. Blauberman, wearing a cream-colored jacket and a cream-and-red striped bow
tie, blended right into it. He was a tall man, with coarse,
black, conspicuously barbered hair, a sharp nose, and a thin-
lipped, dissatisfied mouth. He had deep lines at right angles
to his mouth. His stomach, as he sat, protruded in a medium-

sized paunch. He wore dark-horn-rimmed glasses. He was smoking a slim Dunhill pipe. In years gone by, at hotels and summer resorts, mothers with marriageable daughters had pointed him out to one another as "that gorgeous-looking fella." On the wall behind Dr. Blauberman's head was a Currier & Ives print of a horse-drawn sleigh full of chubby, laughing, red-cheeked, mittened, mufflered, ear-muffed, healthy men, women, and children. On the wall over the couch were framed diplomas, including one from the N.Y.U. College of Medicine, class of 1939. Waiting for Ephraim to speak, Dr. Blauberman crossed and recrossed his legs. "So," he said, finally. And when this produced nothing, he said, "You show your hostility with your silence. Mmmm? Because I say I cannot go on with you as a patient. Yes?"

Dr. Blauberman glanced with discouragement and distaste at the young man on the couch. This was their next-to-last session together. Deadwood. Uncoöperative. Why struggle any more to help him? It was pointless. It was demoralizing. It was leading neither of them anywhere. There were too many sick people waiting to be helped who *wanted* to be helped, whose suitability for psychoanalysis was better. At first, Dr. Blauberman had thought that Ephraim, with his honesty and sincerity and intelligence and what Dr. Blauberman had hoped would turn out to be a classic symptom-neurosis, was extremely suitable. And Dr. Fifield, who had sent Ephraim to him, had thought so, too. But for a whole year now—you could, of course, call the period one of *trial* analysis—using all the technique he had accumulated in years of practice, Dr. Blauberman had been striving to give Ephraim Samuels an awareness of his masochistic self-victimization, and to show him how, by changing his out-look, he could realize himself fully in his music, with his composing and with his clarinet. But there had been no change. And neither had there been a successful transference. Not really. There was no free-associating, and Dr. Blauberman suspected considerable ego regression, reinstating Ephraim's tie to his dead mother. For practically the entire year since his analysis had begun, the previous July, Ephraim had not touched the clarinet, but no analyst would blame Dr. Blauberman for *that*.

He had wanted so much to help this boy, this promising musician, and to set him on the healthy path. He'd been so glad when he got Ephraim as a patient. Ephraim had been such a welcome relief, not only from the dull housewife patients but from the medical profession—the largest category of patients in analysis, according to a recent survey made of psychoanalytic education in the United States. All those doctors, surgeons, social workers, and psychologists. Here was a "gifted" patient. There had been a good deal of discussion lately among Dr. Blauberman's colleagues about "gifted" patients. Dr. Blauberman had never had a really "gifted" patient before. Here was a *musician*. And a musician, moreover, who moved—that is, if Dr. Blauberman could *get* him to move—in the interesting worlds of chamber music and jazz, night clubs and Broadway, as well as Carnegie Hall. Dr. Blauberman was so fascinated by these worlds that, listening to Ephraim, he sometimes forgot about free association and dream interpretation. No harm in that. It was all adding up. Ephraim had even inspired Dr. Blauberman with the idea for a paper to be read at a meeting of the New York Psychoanalytic Society. Dr. Blauberman had actually thought of two appropriate titles: "The Id, the Ego, and the Clarinet" and "An Inquiry Into the Meaning of the Psychodynamics of Musical Composition and the Application of Psychoanalysis to Chamber Music and Jazz, from Bach to Brubeck."

Well. So. Mmmm. That was in the early weeks. Now it was

all one big mess. Transference, that *sine qua non* of analyzability, was now kaput. True, Ephraim had formed a kind of attachment to him. And he had not always been silent, as he was now. He had talked about his relationships with various members of his family, and with various girls; had confided to Dr. Blauberman his modest estimates of his compositions and his involved plans for works he wanted to write in the future; had related all those cozy family anecdotes starring, nine times out of ten, his father, Joseph Samuels; had expressed his passionate enthusiasm for—and made clear his dependence on—his old clarinet teacher, Gustave Lefevre. But they had got nowhere. They hadn't worked a damn thing through. Dr. Blauberman had gone way beyond the call of duty for this boy, but Ephraim wanted to remain tied to his teacher, to his father, to his family. The more Dr. Blauberman heard about the father and the Samuels family, the more fed up he became. The promise of Ephraim as a different kind of patient, and a stimulating one, grew dim. The more Ephraim revealed the family picture, the more familiar and uninteresting it became—the very same sort of people, in fact, that Dr. Blauberman himself had managed to leave so far behind him. There was nothing he didn't know about that world, and he didn't want to be reminded of it any more than he wanted to be pushed back into it. Ephraim, it seemed, did want that very world. Naturally, the reasons were sick reasons, and all of Dr. Blauberman's ingenious ideas and devices for bringing him to act with drive and ambition and get somewhere with himself and with his music were rejected.

During his interneship, in a small Jewish hospital in Brooklyn, not far from the Williamsburg section, where he grew up, Dr. Blauberman had decided he was as smart as the next guy. Maybe he couldn't get an interneship in one of the large, fancy hospitals in Manhattan, but he could measure up alongside any other hospital interne in town. And he knew exactly what he wanted out of life. He wasn't going to be pushed around in medicine as a lousy general practitioner. Not for Al Blauberman a lifelong dependence on the grudged pennies of the Jewish poor. While he was still interning, he divorced the wife he had taken right after he graduated from medical school; she had been nothing but a burden to him and a handicap. She went home to her family. For a while, he received wild telephone calls from her, until he told her family in no uncertain terms that if she continued to bother him he would turn her over to the police. Then he discovered psychiatry. In the veterans' hospitals after the war, he found his experience and tested his hand. This was more like it. No house calls in the middle of the night. No hordes of sufferers pulling and pushing at him. He worked for a while at Bellevue, where he continued to absorb experience; he learned what he could from the European refugees, the devoted disciples of Freud.

"Mmmm?" he said now, around his pipe. "I cannot help you if you don't want to be helped. Yes?"

Ephraim said nothing.

Dr. Blauberman sniffed noisily. What an analyst had to fight against! Nothing came out of this young man, who could have had the whole world if he had only listened to his analyst and let himself be helped. Instead, here he was—sickly, pale, dressed like one of those young Greenwich Village tramps, with soiled, baggy trousers, cheap shoes, sweater, no necktie. The large mouth closed so stubbornly. The blue eyes, so clear, so light, their color undiminished by the

139

dimly lit office. The matted brown hair in need of cutting. The thick, kinky, straw-colored eyebrows. Like his father's, Ephraim had boasted so many times—as though the straw-colored eyebrows were a heritage of great importance.

"Pop is the only man I know who can comb his hair with a towel," Ephraim would say. "He's got this thick hair, the same as mine, and these wild bushy eyebrows, and he never uses a comb—he just gets it fixed up with the towel. That's one thing I've never been able to do. He hates hats, but he's got this old cap he wears that he's had for years—it smells of gasoline. . . . Sometimes I wear a cap. It makes a big hit with girls."

Dr. Blauberman grunted. He himself went in for hats with fancy bands and feathers. As for that father, what he led the family to! The unhealthy sense of values. The denial of society. His children made overdependent. The retardation of Ephraim's emotional development. The lack of drive and ambition to carry the music to fulfillment. They had spent three weeks—fifteen sessions—on Lefevre alone, as Dr. Blauberman demonstrated one way and another how Ephraim was held to the teacher by immature dependence. The running back to the old man, instead of breaking into new territory on his own. And still Ephraim was stubborn. He rejected everything. Negative. Negative. Dr. Blauberman was tired of it. After all, it was only human to want a little reward for your efforts. The analyst's narcissistic gratifications were important, too. Why give and give and give and get nothing, not even a sign of recognition? It wasn't healthy. It wasn't healthy for *anybody*. You had to do what was right for yourself at all times, and in that way you did what was right for the patients. If asked, all his colleagues would agree.

Just the other night, after a meeting of the New York Psy-

140

choanalytic Society, he had stood around waiting impatiently for Harold Seltzer to finish discussing with other colleagues Norman Reider's paper on "Chess, Oedipus, and the Mater Dolorosa." Dr. Blauberman had walked home with Seltzer, who lived near Dr. Blauberman's office, where Dr. Blauberman slept on meeting nights instead of going all the way home to Scarsdale. Seltzer owned a beautiful town house on a side street. Seltzer was no fool. He knew his business. At fifty, Seltzer looked ten years younger. Sailboat Seltzer, he was called, even by patients, who knew he was crazy about sailing. Seltzer escaped from the telephone by the simple expedient of spending long weekends and long vacations on his boat. He always had a tan. He always looked relaxed and happy. He was very popular with the older European analysts and went to all their parties. He was a tremendous rumba dancer and he knew a lot of sailing songs, which he sang in a near-professional baritone voice. He also played the banjo. The Europeans considered him the typical healthy American. He had presented half a dozen papers already at Psychoanalytic Society meetings, on such subjects as "The Id, the Ego, and the Sea" and "Columbus, Narcissism, and the Discovery of America." Seltzer's name was appearing regularly in the indexes of leading psychoanalytic journals. Dr. Blauberman's name had never appeared there even once. Seltzer looked his patients over carefully, and managed to select the ones who could afford to pay thirty-five dollars an hour and up, and give him the least possible inconvenience and bother, as well as a classic and analyzable neurosis. It was important to get patients who came to you five or even six times a week, nicely, quietly, coöperatively, without making a mess, so that from hour to hour you knew where you were. It was important to have patients who were comfortably analyzable from session to session. Dr. Blauberman admired the way Seltzer got the most, in every way, out of his practice.

"Listen, Sailboat, hmmm?" Dr. Blauberman had said. "I've been doing a lot of thinking about criteria for suitability for psychoanalysis. It's a very important question."

"Of course," Seltzer said. "So?"

"I'm thinking of doing a paper on it."

"Blauberman, you know Waldhorn? Mmmm? Waldhorn just *did* a paper on it."

Dr. Blauberman sniffed deeply. "I'll have to read it," he said. "It's a very important question in our work. Do you accept Fenichel's criteria for suitability?"

"Fenichel's. And Freud's."

"How do *you* tell, Sailboat?" Dr. Blauberman said. "About suitability? Mmmm?"

"It ain't so difficult," Seltzer said. "Stay away from the narcissistic neuroses and perverse characters, Blauberman. As you well know, Freud always said they lent themselves poorly to analysis. Yes?"

Dr. Blauberman sighed.

"Don't take it so hard, Blauberman," Seltzer said, laughing. "Hmmm?"

Laughing boy. It was easy enough for him to laugh. Him and his year-round sun tan. "What about Freud's contraindications to suitability, enlarged by Fenichel?" Dr. Blauberman asked.

"Ha!" Seltzer said. "Lack of a reasonable and coöperative ego! Stay away from it! Never take such a case. You have to protect yourself in our work. You know what we mean by ego strength. Right away I spot rigid defenses, I won't even start with them. I should say not. Listen to me, Blauberman.

142

Develop an attitude and stick to it firmly. Remember that Fenichel holds that the crucial factor in determining accessibility is really the dynamic relationship between resistance and the wish for recovery."

"So how do you tell who's suitable for analysis when you don't know them yet?" Dr. Blauberman asked. "Who decides?"

"*You* do, Blauberman."

"Mmmm," Dr. Blauberman said. "After a trial analysis, who is to say suitable or unsuitable? Mmmm?"

"Blauberman, *you* are, mmmm?" Seltzer said, and laughed.

What would Sailboat Seltzer have done with Ephraim, Dr. Blauberman wondered. How would he have dealt with Ephraim's unshakable involvement with his old teacher, Gustave Lefevre?

"I just love the old guy," Ephraim had said. "I'd rather spend a day playing duets with Gus than almost anything."

"So. Mmmm. Two clarinets. Just the two of you. Yes?"

"Oh, man, you just ought to hear the tone Gus gets, even now! At his age!"

Two clarinets. Dr. Blauberman patiently tried to elicit something, anything, from Ephraim on the symbolic significance of the two clarinets. Silence. Nothing. Nowhere. Impossible. If just once he could get Ephraim to react emotionally. The emotion was there, all right. No mistake about it. But Dr. Blauberman couldn't get at it. He tried charm. He tried sympathy. He tried anger. He tried sarcasm. He tried coldness. He tried silence, and usually it was Dr. Blauberman who spoke first. It was very disheartening.

Dr. Blauberman couldn't find anything particularly helpful in his reading. In the hope of getting some elucidation, he looked up an old paper that he recalled his own analyst's hav-

143

ing once made a big fuss over—Franz S. Cohn's "Practical Approach to the Problem of Narcissistic Neuroses," written over twenty years ago. And he read, "There is dull but agitated talking, very rapid without pause, or else scarcely any talk, with long intervals of silence. There is no important difference between these types. In both, thoughts are drifting like a cork on a deep sea of narcissistic libido that presently is going to wash away the analyst." Mmmm? Ephraim Samuels wanted to wash Blauberman away? Very disheartening.

In the beginning, Dr. Blauberman reported enthusiastically to Dr. Fifield during *his* analytic hour (Vertical Position) that Ephraim had a-lot-to-give and could achieve get-well, and that he thought he'd make out satisfactorily with Ephraim—better than he had done with Dr. Fifield's boyhood friend Lester Greenthal. Lester Greenthal's progress, after eight years in analysis with Dr. Blauberman, had been very slight. Lester Greenthal now accused Dr. Blauberman of loving Spencer Fifield more than Lester Greenthal. On the other hand, Marvin Krakower, the pathologist, had made terrific progress. In less than four years, after Marvin Krakower had come to him via Spencer Fifield, the pathologist had married Sally Mandel, the girl Spencer Fifield had been going around with. "Look at Marvin Krakower," Dr. Blauberman was able to tell Spencer Fifield when Fifield was lying on the couch. "Married to Sally. Two lovely children. If you get well, you might have all that." Spencer Fifield, unfortunately, still had a long way to go—chronically intellectualizing patients were, after all, reluctant even to go through the motions of acting on their newly acquired awareness—but he, unlike the deadwood, was working *with* Dr. Blauberman.

Together, Dr. Blauberman and Dr. Fifield had kept Joan Stone, the daughter of Dr. Fifield's wealthiest patient, Hiram

Stone, from eloping with the manager of a neighborhood Christian Science Reading Room. Dr. Fifield had steered her into getting engaged to Barry Rosenblatt, another pathologist Spencer Fifield knew, whose ambition—and he was absolutely unneurotic and open about it—was to marry a rich girl, somebody who would make it economically possible for him to devote his attention fully to science. It had taken plenty out of Dr. Blauberman, the analyst frequently reminded Spencer Fifield, to put Barry Rosenblatt over. That one had been exhausting.

Dr. Blauberman had, in spite of himself, a kind of wistful admiration for some of the older psychoanalysts—especially the Europeans. But they were clannish and snobbish, and tended to treat him in a patronizing manner. They made jokes about life in the suburbs. They occupied prewar-rental apartments on Central Park West—office and home on a single rental—that were filled with the dark-brown, dreary, heavy furniture they had brought with them from Europe. They talked with fervor about "our work." They could afford to make their scholarly, erudite studies in a vacuum. They always seemed to be so lighthearted, so full of humor. They had good appetites. And they were highly sociable, always giving parties. For each other. Dr. Blauberman would hear them talking about their parties at the Psychoanalytic Institute, where he put in his voluntary work with the rest of them. He wasn't invited to their parties, and they seemed to look right through him in the corridors at the Institute or at conventions and conferences. It was apparently simple enough for them to resist being drawn into their patients' neuroses. The analytic discipline they talked so much about was also, it seemed, easy for them. Dr. Blauberman didn't find it easy. Nothing was easy for him. He had to watch his own strength, his own energies, how *much* he gave. If you let them, patients would eat you up. All of you. "Let's face it," Dr. Blauberman said to himself and to his patients. "The neurotic patient is hungry. Mmmm?" And what was the point of letting yourself be eaten up? That was right neither for you nor for your patients. It was debilitating. And the frustration of getting nowhere with a patient was debilitating. After all, Dr. Blauberman was a family man. He had a wife and two children. The children were very popular in their school. His son had just been elected president of his seventh-grade class. Dr. Blauberman worked hard for his living. He wanted something to show for it. He had a lovely sixty-thousand-dollar split-level house in Scarsdale. That was something. This summer, he was going to send both children to one of the finest camps in Vermont. That was something. And he and his wife were going to Spain. That would be something. His father-in-law owned one of the largest laundry chains in the city, and Dr. Blauberman admired him very much. He never saw his own father, who still lived in the section of Brooklyn where Dr. Blauberman had grown up. He didn't bother his father and his father didn't bother him. Like all accredited psychoanalysts, Dr. Blauberman had been psychoanalyzed himself. He was *free* of his father. And of the bitterness and the meanness his father represented. That was something, too.

After disposing of Ephraim Samuels, Dr. Blauberman would be in a position to tackle the problem of what to do about Lester Greenthal. Other Fifield-recommended patients had come and gone, including a young painter who had quit after having tried and failed to commit suicide, and a young strip-teaser who had tried and succeeded. Dr. Blauberman had made his mistakes, but he had learned from them, as he often

146

told his patients, and never made the same mistake twice. His only mistake with Ephraim Samuels had been taking him on in the first place. Still, in the early days things had looked promising.

"And this music you compose," Dr. Blauberman had said at one session. "You will give it to some conductor? Yes? Maybe to Lenny Bernstein?" Dr. Blauberman liked being on a familiar basis with celebrated people his patients talked about.

Ephraim smiled at the ceiling. "I told you, Dr. Blauberman. I'm not ambitious—not that way. Not everybody can be great, man. But I've got a little stuff that's my own. For the time being, I just like to write these little pieces to see what comes out."

"You are afraid. Mmmm?"

"No, it's just that I have to feel my own way by myself for a while, without bringing anyone else into it. At least, not yet."

"So. You are afraid of a rejection. Mmmm?"

"You don't follow, Dr. Blauberman. I just don't want to—"

"I follow more than you think. Why don't you go to this party you are invited to for Lenny?"

"Well, I just don't enjoy those big parties. They're too confusing."

"Are you afraid Lenny or Adolph will reject you?"

"Gosh, no. I like them. They're a lot of fun. But hanging around with them can use up all your time."

"You back away *before* you are rejected. You feel inadequate."

"If I wanted to, I could run around from one party to another, trying to make it with television producers and all that junk. But that isn't what I want."

147

"Lenny Bernstein is on television. Television is good enough for Lenny Bernstein to show millions of people what he can do. Television is a healthy outlet. No?"

"It depends on what you want," Ephraim said.

"Maybe there is something missing in your sense of values about what you want," Dr. Blauberman said.

"Well—" Ephraim began. Then he stopped. As though inspired, he continued, "Here's the way it is, Dr. Blauberman. Last week, I went over to my sister Leah's house for dinner. She's married to Vic, you know, and they have this four-year-old kid, Eugene, named after Eugene Victor Debs—"

"I know, I know," Dr. Blauberman said, impatient with Ephraim's way of breaking into laughter over the child's name.

"I still get a blast out of it, after all these years."

"Mmmm," Dr. Blauberman said, making noises of dissatisfaction.

"What I wanted to tell you," Ephraim went on, "my father was there, too, and Eugene comes over to him and says, 'Grandpa, guess the name of a delicious Jewish drink beginning with the letter A.'"

Dr. Blauberman made further sounds of dissatisfaction. How he loathed these homey stories of the family's self-appreciation.

"So Pop says he gives up, and Eugene screams, 'Ah-malted!'" Ephraim put on an exaggerated Jewish accent. "It turns out that Vic rehearses him in the accent. Vic says he's going to put Eugene on television someday, with Pop's collie, in a new gimmick—a Jewish 'Lassie' program, with Eugene sitting on the dog, relaxed, and telling Jewish jokes. Isn't that wild?" He stopped, realizing that he was getting no response.

"You are not a child," Dr. Blauberman said. "For you, work

in television would be a healthy outlet. You are afraid to engage yourself in the competitive activities in television? Even to the extent of going to a social party?"

"No. You don't get the message, Dr. Blauberman," Ephraim said, in a low voice. "You don't understand. I like to see those people once in a while, but I don't like to run with anybody. I get more pleasure out of talking to my father."

"You go only where it is safe, where you won't be rejected. Yes?"

"Oh, God!" Ephraim said. "I told you. My father is an original, unusual man. I don't know anybody else like him."

Dr. Blauberman made loud sounds of disapproval. "So. At your age. You feel safe only with Papa. You still insist on living with your father. No?"

"Well, sure. Why not? It's not just that he'd be all alone. I *like* being with him. Do you know how he escaped from Siberia? He was—"

"Don't start telling me all that heroic garbage about the Socialists." Dr. Blauberman's anger cut through Ephraim with terrible force. "You won't face the truth about your real feeling about your father. You refuse to admit your hostility to him."

"Well, I've got my beefs and all, but—"

"Why are you so lacking in drive? Why? You don't think it's because of your father? You refuse to admit there is something basically unhealthy about your home situation? *Why* do you stay with him?"

"Pop makes terrific coffee," Ephraim said softly, with a laugh.

"You're twenty-eight. At your age, you should have your own apartment."

"Well, I guess you're right, Dr. Blauberman. And, naturally, when I get married I'll have my own home. But right now I sort of like it where I am. And I can save money. It leaves me free to do my work or anything I please."

"And it gives you an excuse not to compete in the world? To risk letting people hear your music. To sell it. To make some decent money. To be a man. Mmmm?"

"Well—" Ephraim said, and stopped.

One day, Dr. Blauberman had wanted to know why Ephraim played the clarinet in the first place. "The clarinet is basically a symbol, no?" he said. "You prefer an inanimate symbol to real satisfaction. Hmmm. Yes?"

Ephraim laughed. "I like them *both*, Dr. Blauberman. But I do love the clarinet sound. No question about that. It sounds good to me. Of all the musical instruments, the clarinet is closest to nature. It's the tree itself, hollowed out. The sound is *natural.*"

"So. You refuse to face the meaning of the symbolism?"

"Well—" Once more, Ephraim stopped talking.

As time went on, it became clear to Dr. Blauberman that the depression in Ephraim was growing deeper. He evidently felt dissatisfied with himself. He lost interest in the clarinet. After a while, he told Dr. Blauberman he could not enjoy what had been the simple pleasure of sitting down to a quiet supper with his father, or of amusing his small nephews with jazzy tunes on his clarinet. Everything seemed to drop away. So many things had been stirred up into one big hodgepodge in his head. He didn't know where he was. He questioned everything he was and everything he had been doing. He complained to Dr. Blauberman that he couldn't sleep at night. Dr. Blauberman gave him prescriptions for Seconal, to help him sleep. When a single capsule didn't work, he took increasingly large dosages, and showed up at Dr. Blauberman's office still groggy from the effects of Seconal. One day,

Dr. Blauberman announced that there would be no more prescriptions.

"What'll I do, Dr. Blauberman? I can't sleep without it."

"Get it from a physical doctor."

"Dr. Fifield?"

"If he chooses to give it to you."

"But if he doesn't?"

"I can't be responsible for what Dr. Fifield gives you. That is his business. Physical medicine is another department. So."

So. Ephraim went to see Spencer and said he needed Seconal or something to help him sleep. After a few months of giving Ephraim prescriptions for sleeping pills, Spencer, during his analytic hour with Dr. Blauberman, expressed interest over the large amounts of Seconal that Ephraim was consuming. "Frankly, I think he's overintellectualizing, about women and everything, and that's why he can't sleep." Spencer was fresh from the analyst's consideration of Spencer's own tendency to overintellectualize. "Although he denies it, of course, he seems to be opening up. He seems to have made a lot of progress in treatment since that first time I saw him. He had hepatitis, and that leaves you feeling depressed for weeks afterward, but there was more to it than that. Frankly, he needed help if anybody did."

"You really think he is opening up?" Dr. Blauberman said.

"Definitely! He told me he hasn't been able to bring himself to touch the clarinet for months. He says he just doesn't have the wind to blow, and when he tries to play, it makes him feel physically sick. That must show, frankly, that the deep disturbances are rising to the surface. Frankly, I'm sure you're getting somewhere with him."

Dr. Blauberman looked pleased. "So," he said, in a mock-fatherly reproach. "My two siblings are talking about me."

Spencer gave a happy laugh.

"See you tomorrow, mmmm?" Dr. Blauberman said.

And a couple of weeks later Spencer again expressed concern over the sleeping pills Ephraim asked for. "This time, I questioned him about his emotional involvements. I asked him whether he brings up material for you to work with."

"Mmmm," Dr. Blauberman said.

"I asked him whether he had a real relationship with a girl," Spencer went on. He had been chewing over with the analyst his own impoverished relationships with girls. "I really pinned him down and asked him whether his physical needs were being satisfied. I told him he shouldn't be avoiding sexual involvements with emotional content. Mmmm?" he said, giving Dr. Blauberman back his own. "He became upset, very disturbed. He said, 'Who's *avoid*ing anything?' Classical defense-mechanism anger."

Dr. Blauberman sighed.

"I told him psychoanalysis has been extremely helpful to me in my own work," Spencer said stiffly. "Then he asked me whether he ought to have a consultation with Dr. Hans Radelsheim. And I told him he had to bring up *that* question with you. I told him, frankly, it's not a good idea for us in sibling relationships to talk about you with each other."

"I am a psychoanalyst," Dr. Blauberman said to Ephraim at the next-to-last session as Ephraim lay, still not speaking, on the couch. "I don't know how to break you of the Seconal addiction. It is not in my field. You need to go where you can be helped in that respect now."

"Would it be a good idea to have a consultation about what I should do?" Ephraim said, finally talking. "I mean, what I've been trying to figure out is why I got into analysis in the first place. Nothing ever seemed right—now that I think about it—that I tried to do here."

"And whose fault is that?"

"Mine, I guess. But, anyway, my friend Charlie Donato—the bassoonist?—says I ought to have a consultation with this Dr. Hans Radelsheim, you know?"

"Why Radelsheim, hmmm?"

"I don't know. Just because Charlie says he's good, that he knows a lot."

"So. I *don't* know a lot?"

"Well, no. It's just that all I want is to get back to my music. I don't really have a good idea of what's happened to me this past year, and what I should do."

"I am telling you what you should do. You should go to Dr. Fifield and ask him what to do, where to go to be cured of your addiction to Seconal."

"But if I feel worse, should I go to a different *kind* of analyst?"

"If *this* analyst couldn't analyze you at this point, *no* analyst can analyze you," Dr. Blauberman said. "We found that out. At least, not in your present state. Mmmm?"

"Would it hurt just to ask this Dr. Radelsheim about me?"

"There is no reason to call Radelsheim. I have nothing to ask Radelsheim." He stood up from his chair. "See you tomorrow."

That night, at another meeting of the Psychoanalytic Society, Dr. Blauberman sat next to Sailboat Seltzer, who was sitting next to Dr. Abe Letkin, one of the old-timers—one of the oldest practitioners of analysis in town, as a matter of fact. Letkin didn't let anybody ever forget it, either. He always irritated Dr. Blauberman, with all his *gemütlich*, good-natured, relaxed ways—the Middle European Barry Fitzgerald of psychoanalysis. Once, Dr. Blauberman telephoned Letkin about a clinic patient, and Letkin took the opportu-

153

nity to make one of his speeches, lecturing Dr. Blauberman about how Freud was a saint, a poet, and a philosopher, not a scientist. When Dr. Blauberman tried to get a word in edgewise, Letkin said he had to go, and cut him off with a "Lotsa luck." Letkin's signoff was always "Lotsa luck." Some dignified way for one of the elders of psychoanalysis to speak! But, for reasons Dr. Blauberman could not understand, Letkin was admired and respected by all the big wheels in the Psychoanalytic Society. Why? All he did was make cracks about the stuffiness, the narrow-mindedness, the limitations, the godlike pretensions, the shortcomings of analysts—particularly some of the younger analysts, who, according to Letkin, were constitutionally unfitted for the work they tried to do. In the discussion that followed the reading of a paper at a meeting, Letkin would get up and try to turn it into philosophical channels. Philosophical channels bored Dr. Blauberman. And it wasn't as though Letkin's views came as a surprise to his listeners. Every time he got up to talk about Freud's really *significant* qualities, his *spiritual* qualities, he would be received with affectionate groans. "Leanness," Letkin would say, with the kind of inflection Dr. Blauberman always found so embarrassing. "Leanness and asceticism constituted Freud's ego-ideal." And everybody would look at Letkin as though he were *the* father symbol. It was infuriating. Dr. Blauberman sometimes wished he had the nerve to get up and say something about it.

Before the meeting was called to order, Letkin was talking, in a conspiratorial, laughing manner, to Sailboat Seltzer. Letkin was saying what a terrible collection of paintings had been donated to the Psychoanalytic Society for its art show to raise money for the Psychoanalytic Institute. "I tell you, Sellbought, instead of throwing out these lousy paintings by name painters, they give them to *psychoanalysts* to sell. That is what they think of psychoanalysts."

And Seltzer said, putting the Letkinese on thick, "A rummage sale is a rummage sale by anybody, no?"

It happened that Dr. Blauberman and his wife had picked up an Abstract Expressionist painting by a well-known painter for only three hundred and ninety-five dollars at the art show, and it was now hanging in their living room in Scarsdale. Dr. Blauberman started to tell them about it, but Letkin was inviting Seltzer to come to a party. Letkin was saying, "Sellbought, don't forget to bring your banjo. The food will be good, and we have lotsa whiskey."

"Letkin, by me you are the A No. 1 host among analysts," Seltzer said. That Seltzer! What he wouldn't do to make himself popular with Letkin and the other old-timers!

Letkin clapped Seltzer on the back. "Let me tell you a new Myron Cohen joke I just heard from one of my patients," he said to Seltzer, extending his attention to Dr. Blauberman with one brief eyewink and then turning back to Seltzer.

"So tell me already," Seltzer said, still putting on the schmalzy act to ingratiate himself with Letkin.

"So," Letkin began. "This patient comes to the analyst and lies down on the couch, and the analyst says to him, 'You've got to stop smoking.' 'That'll help me?' the patient asks. And the analyst says, 'Yes, you're burning the couch.'"

Letkin and Seltzer killed themselves laughing. Two laughing boys.

The meeting was called to order. There was a long paper read by Kurt Eissler and entitled "Notes on the Environment of a Genius." It was about Goethe and Goethe's loving father. Just what Dr. Blauberman needed! Not only another of those esoteric studies but one about loving fathers. At the meeting

155

before, it was Radelsheim—one of those self-appointed saints regarded with awe by so many of the other analysts—on the psychic function of artistic compulsion. Tonight, Dr. Blauberman noticed Radelsheim sitting at the other side of the room, absorbed, rapt, listening attentively to Eissler. Radelsheim and his original theories. But it was Blauberman who had to deal with the environmental setup of an Ephraim Samuels. In the discussion that followed the presentation of the paper, Eissler said that analysts possibly are not too well prepared to deal psychoanalytically with situations in which parents might have a good effect on their children rather than the opposite. That was a big help. Everybody gave one of those arrogantly humble laughs of self-understanding. The hypocrites! Tomorrow morning, most of them would be struggling, like him, against resistance reinforced from the outside.

This time, Letkin, thank God, didn't make his usual speech. He was too busy laughing it up with Seltzer. Dr. Blauberman hung around with them, listening glumly to Letkin make disrespectful cracks about Goethe.

"Eissler should have explained why Goethe didn't know how to laugh at himself," Letkin was saying. "Goethe had no humor. Tell me, Sellbought. What kind of father gives issue to a son who does not know how to laugh at himself?"

Seltzer gave a chuckle instead of an opinion. Sailboat Seltzer always played it safe.

Dr. Blauberman tried to get in on the amusement. "Eissler you couldn't call exactly a Myron Cohen, mmmm?"

Letkin gave him a cool look and said, "I thought Eissler brought out some brilliant points, Blauberman."

"On the question of neutralized energy," Seltzer said. "For

Goethe, creating, Eissler pointed out, was one of the deepest instinctual processes, mmmm?"

And Letkin said, "The environment that was beneficial for Goethe could, with someone else, have led to vastly different results, possibly delinquency or psychosis? I agree with Eissler."

"Mmmm?" Dr. Blauberman said. "Mmmm." He wanted to ask Letkin what he thought about an Ephraim Samuels. What about the resistance of an Ephraim Samuels, thanks to one of those loving fathers? But the hell with it. All these people were too busy becoming saints, developing original theories, writing papers. Dr. Blauberman thought fleetingly about "The Id, the Ego, and the Clarinet." The hell with that, too. There were more important things.

The next morning, Dr. Blauberman had two very difficult sessions in a row—first with Joan Stone, who tried to pull a sudden flip-flop in her somewhat unstable feelings about Barry Rosenblatt, and then with Lester Greenthal, who decided that day to spring on Dr. Blauberman the idea that *he* should have a consultation with some other analyst. Dr. Blauberman got Lester Greenthal quieted down. After Lester Greenthal had left, Dr. Blauberman picked up his telephone and called Mr. Samuels at his place of business, a one-man auto-repair shop in Long Island City.

"Mr. Samuels?"

"Yes, *sir*." The father had a slight Eastern European accent, and his "sir" was used not as a respectful salutation but as a form of emphasis.

"Mr. Joseph Samuels?"

"Yes, *sir*."

"Dr. Blauberman here. I'm informing you of the termination of my treatment of your son. . . . Did you hear?" Dr. Blauberman asked impatiently. "I'm discharging my obligations with this telephone call. Your son's last appointment with me will be today."

"Dr. *Blau*berman?" Mr. Samuels asked nervously, uncertainly, as though he were surprised to have proof suddenly that there *was* a Dr. Blauberman. "Is Ephraim all right, Dr. Blauberman?" He enunciated his words with care.

"He's supposed to be here for his last hour this afternoon— if he shows up," Dr. Blauberman said. "I'm afraid I can't do anything any more for your son. I can't carry him any more. I've knocked myself out for him. He just refuses to work his problems out."

"But, Dr. Blau—"

"He refuses to let himself be helped. You can't help a patient who doesn't want to be helped."

"What's all it about?" Mr. Samuels sounded terrified. He couldn't get his words out in order.

"What—it—is—all—about," Dr. Blauberman said, demonstrating extreme patience, "is simply that your son is too sick to be treated by an analyst. . . . Look, I can't spend all this time talking on the telephone. I've got a lot of sick people to see."

"Ephraim thinks the world of you," Mr. Samuels said. "He hasn't taken an interest in anything else for a whole year. Does he want to stop seeing you?"

Irritability with this slow-talking, slow-thinking man began to grow in Dr. Blauberman, but he gave a laugh and said, "Does any patient want to stop seeing the *analyst?*"

The humor seemed to be lost on Mr. Samuels. "What is the matter with my son?" he was asking, in a quavery voice. "Can you tell me—"

158

"I've got to hang up," Dr. Blauberman interrupted. "Sorry. If you insist on discussing this, I'll give you an appointment. This afternoon? At two-fifty? Mmmm?"

"Well—" Mr. Samuels began.

"It's the hour following your son's. Yes?"

"Yes."

"Be here, please. Two-fifty." Dr. Blauberman hung up.

How many times in the past had he tried to get Ephraim to face the reality of what Mr. Samuels was: a neurotic, frightened, dominating figure, hanging on to the past, keeping his son tied to his own self-limiting fears of society. Always, Ephraim had denied it.

Dr. Blauberman had finally said one day, "If your father is so wise, why don't you go to *him* with your problems? Why do you come to me at all?"

"But Dr. Fifield said I needed treatment," Ephraim said. "And you said I needed it, too. Pop doesn't want to interfere with the analysis or anything else I'm trying to do for myself. But I can see he's worrying about me. He can't understand why I don't play the clarinet any more or see any friends or girls. Not that he ever says anything."

"Hmmm. So you were so well adjusted and happy, and you were realizing yourself so fully, *before* you came to analysis, mmmm?" Dr. Blauberman asked.

"Well, no. I've always had this—this—nature, sort of quiet and sad," Ephraim said. "I told you, my mother was always that way, too."

"Mmmm," Dr. Blauberman said.

"I got hit with hepatitis just as I was starting on this project of transposing for clarinet the viola and violin parts of some Bach suites. I was working day and night on them

159

with old Gus Lefevre. Did I tell you he wrote that basic book of instruction I began with as a kid?"

"Mmmm." If it wasn't the father he was holding on to, it was the old teacher.

"It really got me down," Ephraim said, "having to give up working with Gus. That's when Dr. Fifield told me I ought to consult you."

"So. Maybe it was a good thing you had to give up working with Gus," Dr. Blauberman said.

"Good!" Ephraim cried out in horror. "It wasn't *good*, man. You ought to see Gus. He's retired now, in his seventies, living with his wife in this little cottage deep in the woods, way out on Long Island. I used to get up at dawn to travel three hours each way on the Long Island Rail Road just for the privilege of playing duets with Gus. I used to get up before *Pop*, and he's been getting up every morning at six. For the past fifty years. And I'm a guy who likes his sleep."

"And you stayed overnight at the teacher's house?" Dr. Blauberman asked. "You looked there for another home. Yes?"

"Sure it's home!" Ephraim cried again. "You ought to hear Gus. We'd stay up until four in the morning playing Bach, with only his wife for an audience. We'd make tape recordings of two parts, and then play two other parts along with the tapes. You ought to hear that sound. Four clarinets. It was wild. Mrs. Lefevre couldn't make Gus go to bed. You ought to hear him blow. He's almost three times my age, and I could barely keep up with him."

Dr. Blauberman said, "Not two clarinets but *four*. Yes? Do you think you know what it means, the four?"

Ephraim looked puzzled, and uninterested in numbers. "Once, I brought the tapes back and played them for Pop,"

160

he went on. "You know what he said? He said, 'It's beautiful, Eephie; it does my heart good to listen.' That's the way he talks, you know? He's been so lost and miserable ever since my mother died, and yet he can get a blast out of hearing me play."

"Why four?" Dr. Blauberman said, trying to bring him back on the track. "You think you know why you like four?"

Another thing Dr. Blauberman had tried repeatedly to accomplish with Ephraim was to make him aware of the deeper significance of his careless attitude toward money. He was so satisfied to drift along, making a few dollars here and there playing clarinet at school dances or trade-union parties, at resort hotels or small clubs in the Village. It was clear to Dr. Blauberman that the lack of drive to make money came directly from Mr. Samuels. Ephraim told him about it almost boastfully.

"Pop has just never been really *interested* in money, and he's always hated what so many other men have to do in order to earn big money," Ephraim told him. "When my mother was alive, she'd say how nice it would be to have a good set of dishes or stuff like that, but her heart wasn't really in it, either. You know what Pop always told us?"

Dr. Blauberman was silent. He despised what Pop always told them.

"Pop always said, 'As long as I have these two hands, we will never go hungry. We will always make out.' And we always did make out." Ephraim held his own hands open before him, the fingers spread out. His hands were long, the fingers tapered, the skin rough and flat at the tips from years of pressing clarinet keys.

"You made out?" Dr. Blauberman said. "You think your father makes out?"

161

"Well, he misses my mother," Ephraim said slowly. "If you know what I mean, Dr. Blauberman.

"No. What *do* you mean?"

"Well, he misses her deeply. And the way he says it— remembering her face still makes it impossible, after three years, for him to look fully into the face of any other woman."

"So. He holds on to you. Yes? He insists on living in the old apartment? With you?"

"He keeps his sorrow to himself," Ephraim said. "He doesn't try to put anything off on me."

"He sees other women now? He has friends? Mmmm?"

"Well, no. He never needed many people. He never did a lot of running around. My mother was the same way. He's got his dog," Ephraim said, his voice lifting in sudden delight. "This four-month-old collie. Silky. He's a beautiful puppy. The first dog he's had in ten years. We used to have a retriever—he died in Pop's arms at the age of *twenty*. It took Pop ten whole years before he could bring himself to get another dog. That's the way he is."

"And that's enough?" Dr. Blauberman said. "A dog?"

"The collie is this beautiful sable-and-white puppy, so affectionate and intelligent," Ephraim said. "Pop loves that puppy."

"So," Dr. Blauberman said. "Your father doesn't have a housekeeper for the apartment where you live—in— Where is it, did you say?"

"Jackson Heights."

"Yes." Dr. Blauberman couldn't bring himself to pronounce the name. How he hated the thought of anyone's wanting to remain in Jackson Heights. He had the complete family picture by this time, and to him it was not exhilarating: The eldest child, Leah, married to the trade-union organizer Vic-

162

tor Fine, with their four-year-old boy, Eugene Victor, named after Debs. The elder son, Barney, married to Terry, with a fifteen-month-old baby, Jimmy. Mr. Samuels managing all his own housekeeping in the apartment he shared with Ephraim and the dog.

But Ephraim insisted on bringing the picture into sharper focus. Dr. Blauberman indulged him and listened.

"Pop gets up every morning at six o'clock sharp, without any assistance from any alarm clock. He always makes the same breakfast for himself. Freshly squeezed orange juice. It's got to be freshly squeezed. Two soft-boiled eggs. Percolated coffee, with heavy cream and four teaspoons of sugar. Four slices of white bread with sweet butter. To Pop, white bread is a delicacy. He was born in this muddy village in pre-Revolutionary Russia. When he was just a boy in his late teens, he was exiled to Siberia and escaped to America, and so white bread to him is very special, it sort of represents—"

"All right, all right, I know that," Dr. Blauberman interrupted.

"He always leaves the white bread on the kitchen table for me," Ephraim continued, in a lower voice. "He always squeezes enough orange juice for me and leaves a large glass of it for me next to the bread. He always leaves the coffeepot for me on the stove. Then he feeds Silky and sets out in this old Plymouth sedan of his for his auto-repair shop. And Silky goes along, sitting in the front seat with him, just as Blackie always used to do."

"Yes, yes," Dr. Blauberman said. "So?"

"So that's the way he is, that's all. He's got this little yard behind his shop, for Silky to wander around in. He's got this corny picture of Abraham Lincoln hanging over his desk, and right next to it a picture of Eugene Victor Debs. He's got this big picture window in the front of his shop, that he installed with his own hands. He's got this big collection of potted plants in front of the window, that he started with my mother before I was born. Our house is full of plants, and Leah's whole living room is full of them, too. She keeps telling Pop the neighbors think she's crazy."

"So. The neighbors think she is neurotic, your sister?"

As though Dr. Blauberman had made a joke, Ephraim laughed. "Silky moseys about or sleeps near the plants at the shop," he said. "Pop loves having Silky with him there. You know Pop offered the puppy to me the other day? He saw me feeling so low, I think he wanted to cheer me up or something. . . . It's crazy, but Pop treats almost everything as though it were alive. You know, he really *loves* automobiles? You know, he always refers to a car in the feminine gender?"

"Mmmm," Dr. Blauberman said.

"And what he loves to do especially, even when cars look alike or are built alike, is to discover their individual differences, as though they were alive."

"The automobile is inanimate," Dr. Blauberman said. "The clarinet is inanimate. Yes?"

At one point, Dr. Blauberman had tried to determine how the Samuels family felt about Ephraim's career. Nobody else in the family was musical. Nobody else in the family was "gifted."

"Pop loves to listen to me play," Ephraim had said. "That is, he *used* to love to listen to me play when I still played. You know, he really gets the message in jazz? He loves to hear me play Mozart, but, believe it or not, he really gets a blast out of jazz. He really swings. Once, he came down to this dump I played in, the Zero Inn, in the Village. It was

164

wild. Pop had never seen anything like it, and he was blushing all over the place, seeing all the chicks in pants and stuff. You know the way they dress. Then I started playing with Josh Leonard, the pianist. And I was tossing a Monk thing back and forth with Josh, and then, while Josh laid down a foundation, I blew a brand-new melodic line about a mile long, and I could see Pop's face while I played. He was excited, and I could see him bouncing with the beat. Man, what a sight!"

"So. Your father holds on to you, lives through you?"

"You don't get the message, Dr. Blauberman. He just likes to listen to me play. One hot, sweltering Sunday, I felt like staying home to practice. Pop likes to read the Sunday *Times* or play with my nephews when they visit, while I practice runs or just test reeds. That's the way he is. This one hot Sunday, it was so damn hot I took off everything except my shorts and sat around barefoot, whittling down a reed. You know, he just sat there with me, watching until I got that reed down to the exact thickness I wanted. You know why? Because he was interested. And you should have seen his face when I got the damn reed done right."

"You feel separated from him? You feel you are an individual in your own right?"

"Well, Pop is a big lemonade drinker," Ephraim said. "So I got to be one, too. I guess that's a great example of how unseparated from him I am. Whenever I'm practicing, he always makes a large pitcher of cold lemonade and leaves it handy for me to get at. Then he'll retire and read a book and listen to me practice, while I try to perfect a single run or something like that. He likes to hear me do runs as much as anything else. Once, I went over to him after I had swabbed out the clarinet, and showed him my sore, bruised underlip.

165

I did it because I knew he'd get such a blast out of it. And I said, 'It's the wound of battle. I'm winning. I'm beginning to feel like the boss.' And you know what he said? He said, 'That's nice, Eephie,' and then he was so embarrassed and short of breath he stuck his head in the refrigerator pretending to look for something to eat for supper."

"So maybe your father should go to an analyst, to wean him away from *you*, yes?"

"Oh, God!" Ephraim said with a sigh.

" 'Oh, God,' but you don't do anything with your music. You don't realize yourself in any way. You don't play. You think that is healthy?"

"The way I feel lately, I don't want to play," Ephraim said.

"You do not face the reality of your relationship with your father. You resist the transference relationship with me. How can I help you if you do not want to be helped?"

"I just want to get back to the music," Ephraim said.

"And you will play at little Socialist meetings with your music?" Dr. Blauberman said sarcastically. "You will bury yourself in obscurity? Yes?"

"I told you, Pop was a Socialist when we were kids," Ephraim said. "But even then he always argued with the Socialists, too; he said they were too narrow-minded. He's never been able to go with any single group."

"He is too good for society, mmmm?" Dr. Blauberman said.

"He's in a class by himself," Ephraim said. "There's always been some idea or some feeling that would make him hold to himself, no matter what anybody else was saying or doing."

"He goes his own way and you want to follow?" Dr. Blauberman said. "The way of self-victimization."

Talk about environmental resistances. No analyst could work with a patient against such a neurotic, dominating

166

father. In a way, though, he was glad he had telephoned Mr. Samuels. It was unorthodox, but it was a goddam generous, as well as smart, thing to do.

A few minutes before the beginning of Ephraim Samuels' last session, Dr. Blauberman received a telephone call from Dr. Hans Radelsheim.

"Blauberman? Radelsheim."

"Oh, yes, I saw you at the meeting last night. I didn't have a chance to say hello. It was an interesting paper, I thought, Eissler's paper on—"

"Yes. Blauberman, I'm calling about the boy Ephraim Samuels. You are discontinuing treatment of him?"

"Well, yes and no," Dr. Blauberman said. "As far as suitability for analysis goes—"

"But you are discontinuing? The boy says you do not wish to treat him any more."

"You know you can't get an objective picture from the patient," Dr. Blauberman said with a little muffled laugh. "This boy is very disturbed, Radelsheim, mmmm? Narcissistic neurosis. The transference relationship—"

Again Radelsheim cut him off. "These cases are very difficult. But you have dismissed him as your patient?"

The superior bastard. Who did he think he was? Dr. Blauberman said angrily, "I have a session with him this afternoon. I'm seeing the father. The father is—"

"Yes, Blauberman. Could you tell me, please—did you terminate the treatment?"

"Yes, Radelsheim. I've decided to let the boy go, for the time being."

"All right. I'll see what I can do for him."

"The boy is in subjection to his father and incapable of

transferring his libido to a new sexual object," Dr. Blauberman said in a rush. "In reaction to his infantile—"

"Thanks very much. I'll see him." And Radelsheim hung
up.

"Why don't you sit on the couch today?" Dr. Blauberman
said when Ephraim showed up for his last session. "No need
to lie down. We're not going to be bringing up any material
today. Yes?" He leaned back in his chair, and started to put
fresh tobacco in his pipe. Ephraim sat on a corner of the
couch. He had a self-conscious, uncomfortable smile on his
face. Dr. Blauberman saw resentment there, and accusation,
and strain. He brushed the tobacco crumbs off his lap. Then
he put a cigarette lighter to his pipe, and, after a brief struggle, gave it up in favor of a lighted match.

"Well," Ephraim said. "I guess you know I went to see Dr.
Radelsheim."

"Hmmm." Dr. Blauberman, having successfully lit the
pipe, puffed a lot of smoke.

"Didn't he call you?" Ephraim asked. "He said he was going to call you."

"He called, he called."

"He says he'll see me, if you're not going to treat me any
more."

"If I couldn't analyze you, no analyst can analyze you,"
Dr. Blauberman said. "If you have so much of your own
money to throw away finding out that another analyst can
do nothing with you, that is up to you. Mmmm? But I have
seen you for a year. I know what you should do."

"Well—" Ephraim said.

"You need to go somewhere for a rest."

"Well—" Ephraim said.

"Perhaps someday you may want to try analysis again,"

168

Dr. Blauberman said. "In that case"—Dr. Blauberman paused and gave what was meant to be a fatherly smile— "I'll be happy to talk things over with you again. Maybe in a year or so. Mmmm?"

"I don't think so," Ephraim said, blushing. "As a matter of fact, Dr. Radelsheim said—"

"I don't need to hear what Dr. Radelsheim said," Dr. Blauberman said. "I have talked to Dr. Radelsheim myself. I don't think you are in a position to understand what Dr. Radelsheim is saying."

Ephraim looked astonished. "Dr. Radelsheim was awfully nice to me," he said. "He talked to me for almost two hours."

Oh, that bastard and his big mouth! "You must realize that a person in your position will hear only what he *wants* to hear," Dr. Blauberman said. "Don't you think that I am a little better qualified to understand Dr. Radelsheim than you are? Mmmm?"

"But he didn't think I should—"

Dr. Blauberman sat forward and made impatient noises. "You went against my advice in going to see Dr. Radelsheim," he said. "I warned you that you would become confused."

Ephraim was silent for a few moments, and Dr. Blauberman relaxed in his chair and puffed.

"But he says it's important for me to get back to my music," Ephraim said. "And that's all I care about!"

"All?" Dr. Blauberman asked.

"I'm a musician, man!" Ephraim said.

"Of course," Dr. Blauberman said indulgently. "It is important at this point that you just rest, and then get back to your clarinet. And there is no need for you to go running around to any more analysts. Mmmm?"

"Well, I told Dr. Radelsheim I'd come to see him until I

got going again with my music," Ephraim said. "That is, he said he would be available if I wanted him."

"There is no need to see Radelsheim any more," Dr. Blauberman said. He cleared his throat. "Your father wanted to come in to see me today. So I agreed to see him here. It's unusual procedure, but I thought you might like it."

"*Me?*"

"You talk so much about your father—you don't want him to meet your analyst?" Dr. Blauberman said.

"Are you still my analyst?"

"Of course. I will not be treating you for a while, but once you choose an analyst, there is something of the analyst that stays with you always." He smiled at the young man. "Your father should be here soon. I will be glad to meet him."

"What do you want to do, analyze *Pop?*"

Dr. Blauberman got up from his chair. "I'll just go out and see if your father is here," he said.

He opened the door of his inner office and went out to his spacious waiting room. Through the eighteen-foot unbroken spread of window facing the park, the sun was flooding into the room. It had taken years, years of hard work and effort and giving of himself to his patients, to get that room. The room had a brand-new Old American look. Thick hooked rugs, a ladder-back maple rocking chair with a calico cotton cushion tied onto the seat, a black Boston rocker, and half a dozen Currier & Ives prints on the walls. A very low lowboy held stocks of modern, shiny magazines, including *Réalités*. The interior decorator had worked out every last little detail directly with him and Mrs. Blauberman until they had precisely what they wanted.

He pushed the magazines on the lowboy into two neat stacks. A vague sensation of fear touched at his stomach, as

170

it always did when he looked around that room. Because he had such keen self-awareness, Dr. Blauberman was not surprised. He was, in fact, accustomed to this sensation. But someday that would be gone, too, and then he would be able to enjoy the room.

As he returned to the inner office and was about to close the door, he caught a glimpse of Mr. Samuels arriving, the soiled gray cap on his head. Exactly what Dr. Blauberman had expected! The dreariness of it all! Christ! And the whole damn family seemed to have come along. Leah, the young woman must be; and her husband, Victor Fine; and the other son, Barney. Victor Fine wore a blue denim work shirt with a maroon knit tie. Nobody in the family knew how to dress! Barney, the good-natured one, who worked in the Washington produce market at night, had on brown corduroy slacks and a red-and-white checked gingham sports shirt open at the collar. The family neurosis in diagram! Dr. Blauberman left the door open a crack, and watched the father sit down in the Boston rocker, unrocking. The father took out a large steel pocket watch and nodded to the others; they had made it on time.

Opening the door all the way, his pipe between his teeth, Dr. Blauberman said, "Come in."

Mr. Samuels, his son, his daughter, and his son-in-law stood up.

"*All* of you?" Dr. Blauberman's smile was forgiving. He didn't move from the doorway as he looked the group over more closely: Leah, very serious and respectful, wearing a wrinkled wool dress with an unfashionable hemline; her husband's obvious belligerence; the brother's open, untroubled face; Mr. Samuels in his badly fitting suit and curling collar, with his rough hands and paint-stained fingernails.

171

"Ephraim?" Mr. Samuels asked. "Is Ephraim here?"

"Yes, he's here." Dr. Blauberman sighed. "In here." He led the way inside and, lowering the foot of his chair with a lever, sat down.

Ephraim looked embarrassed as his family trooped in. Mr. Samuels went over to him and put a hand on his son's shoulder. "Hello, Eephie," he said.

"Hello, Pop. What you want to come way over here for?" Mr. Samuels shrugged.

"Well, sit down, be seated," Dr. Blauberman said, with a kind of cozy cordiality. "You"—he nodded at Victor Fine and, taking the pipe from his mouth, pointed the stem at one of his slat-back armchairs—"sit there."

Vic sat there. Mr. Samuels sat down on the couch next to Ephraim, and the two others squeezed in alongside.

"Where'd you leave Silky, anyway, Pop?" Ephraim asked.

"He's right outside, Eeph!" Vic said quickly and in an unnaturally loud voice.

"Here?" Ephraim shouted. "*Here?*"

Mr. Samuels blushed. He looked at Dr. Blauberman and smiled.

"Tied to the umbrella stand outside, Eephie," Leah said.

"Oh, my God!" Ephraim said, and started to laugh. His father gave him a proud look and then turned expectantly to the Doctor.

"Pop didn't want to leave the puppy alone in the car," Leah said to Dr. Blauberman.

"The puppy is like a little baby," Mr. Samuels said. "Would you leave a baby alone? Somebody might break into the car and take him."

"I hope it doesn't look as though we do things neurotically," Leah said.

"It's not neurotically," her husband said.

"I mean, dragging a collie like that all over the city," Leah said. "That puppy is going to grow up to be a big dog. Normally, he'd be on a farm, out in the fields, minding the sheep or something. It might look neurotically to some people. Not to me. But that's the way we might look to other people."

"Leah's the expert on all this psychological stuff," Barney said to Dr. Blauberman.

Dr. Blauberman felt like rapping a gavel for order. "This shouldn't take too long," he began crisply. "Actually, meeting with you is a highly unusual procedure, but I happened to have the free hour"—he nodded graciously to Ephraim— "and your father wanted to come in, so"—he nodded graciously to Mr. Samuels—"here we are. I didn't know I was getting a delegation. Safety in numbers, mmmm? Well, you're all here. I've heard a lot about you." He looked from Mr. Samuels to his sons, to his daughter, to his son-in-law, and then singled Leah out to direct his remarks to. "The fact is that Ephraim and I have reached an impasse." These people wouldn't know what an impasse was, but let it go. "Our relationship just hasn't worked out. Perhaps it's my fault"— Dr. Blauberman gave a small, self-disparaging laugh—"and perhaps it's because Ephraim refuses to do his part. He's wasting his time and mine. And he's wasting your money, Mr. Samuels."

Mr. Samuels half stood up from the couch and opened his mouth to say something. Ephraim pulled him down to the couch. Dr. Blauberman was still talking. "Frankly, Ephraim is lazy, yes? But that isn't what is our concern of the moment. That's neither here nor there." He paused and chewed on the stem of his pipe. "You must be aware," he

173

went on, concentrating his attention on Leah, "that Ephraim is a disturbed young man. He has become—you might say—addicted to a powerful barbiturate. He takes tremendous quantities of Seconal every night. He has become stalemated. Unable to move in any direction." Dr. Blauberman looked straight into Mr. Samuels' face and pointed his pipestem at him. "After today, I cannot take any further responsibility in this case. I've tried and tried to help your son, Mr. Samuels. I've tried to get him to use his gifts to make something of himself in life, but I'm sorry to say he prefers to remain—a slob." He gave a kidding little laugh.

Mr. Samuels looked wildly at Ephraim, and then around at the members of his family. Ephraim smiled his self-conscious smile. Between great agitated gasps of breath, Mr. Samuels said, "He is an angel. Don't you know that this boy is an angel?"

"Take it easy, Pop," Ephraim said.

"Ephraim and I have been through all this over and over again," Dr. Blauberman said. "Isn't that right, Ephraim? So. We're not here for a *Kaffeeklatsch* now, are we? Who has time to sit around chatting? I have a lot of sick people to see. Mmmm? Much as I'm flattered by this family committee visit." He looked at his wristwatch. The faster he got these people out of his office, the better for everybody. He hadn't gone into medicine to be surrounded by Joseph Samuels & Co. What strength it took to maintain a casual, professional manner with them when all he wanted to do was to say please, just go away and don't bother me! He wanted air. Air! People of this kind always seemed to be asking for help or sympathy or something, and they never had anything to offer in return. They all sat there, the bunch of them, with their irritating innocence, accusing him of God knows what. "We won't con-

174

sider this a regular hour," he said pleasantly. "You people have paid out enough in medical bills already. Yes?" He tried to smile at Mr. Samuels. The smile worked at the corners of his mouth and died. "So. Ephraim will go to a little hospital for a while and get a nice long rest. Yes?"

"Rest?" Mr. Samuels cried. "You say *rest?* In a *hospital?*"

Dr. Blauberman smiled at Leah and said calmly, "Eephie needs to get over taking Seconal—sleeping pills. He can do that best in a hospital. A rest home, if you will." He looked ostentatiously at his watch.

"Where do you want Eephie to go?" Leah asked. Her eyes filled with tears. She didn't even have a decent handkerchief, Dr. Blauberman noticed; she held a rolled-up ball of damp Kleenex to her face. If he let them, this family would eat him up. Oh, how Sailboat Seltzer, that bastard, would run!

"That I can't tell you," he said. "Eephie . . . Ephraim has his physical doctor, Dr. Fifield. Dr. Fifield will make arrangements for where Ephraim should go. . . . Well. That's it." Dr. Blauberman started to get out of his chair.

"No!" Mr. Samuels cried. "I say *no!* Eephie used to play the clarinet. The Doctor tells him he needs to go to a psychoanalyst, and all the trouble starts." Mr. Samuels was shouting. With the windows open, he was noisy enough to be heard by the doorman downstairs, or quite possibly by Sailboat Seltzer a couple of blocks away. Christ! This emotional old man! What a mistake! He'd never make a mistake like this one again!

"Eephie used to play—it was beautiful," Mr. Samuels said. "The Mozart. The Concerto for Clarinet. He was playing parts of it for my wife and me when he was twelve."

"The trouble started when Eephie goes to Dr. Fifield for his hepatitis," Barney said. "Freddy—that concert pianist on

175

the duo-piano team of Freddy and Eddy—sent him to Dr. Fifield."

"*That* is when the trouble started?" Dr. Blauberman said, but his sarcasm escaped Barney.

"Yes," Barney said earnestly. "Dr. Fifield wanted to go to concerts with Eephie and stuff. And before we knew it, he was sending Eephie to a psychoanalyst—the same one he goes to himself."

"So," Dr. Blauberman said, and sniffed. This simple-minded brother was a real prize.

"Eephie used to play all the time!" Mr. Samuels shouted. "Now there's nothing!"

"He was terrific on all that chamber music," Barney said.

"Eephie sounds as good as Benny Goodman," Leah said.

"*Nobody* sounds as good as Benny Goodman," Vic said, "but if anybody sounds as good as Benny Goodman it's Eephie."

"Look—" Dr. Blauberman began.

"What happened?" Mr. Samuels shouted. "Tell me what happened!"

"Mr. Samuels," Dr. Blauberman said. "I would do anything I could to help your boy. But I've tried. He doesn't want to coöperate. I'm afraid there's nothing I *can* do. I'm really sorry."

"You told Eephie he had to be more aggressive. Why? Why does Eephie have to be more aggressive?" Mr. Samuels went on, still shouting. "Nobody ever thought he had to be more aggressive."

"Pop never pushed us to do anything we didn't want to do," Barney said. He, too, was speaking at the top of his voice. "Pop doesn't believe in that."

Dr. Blauberman tried to remember whether he had ever

176

called his own father "Pop," even when he was a boy, but he couldn't remember.

"I know a patient sometimes has to be set back before he can move forward," Leah said. "But we don't care about those other things—about whether or not he should be more aggressive and all that. We just like Eephie the way he is. We just want him to be happy."

"Eeph was making out," Barney said. "He belonged to the musicians' union and played for union rates. He was playing jazz in some of those Village places. He put a lot of effort into his composing."

"Ladies and gentlemen!" Dr. Blauberman said. "I can't sit around with you, arguing this way. All I'm trying to tell you, Mr. Samuels, is that—"

"What will Eephie do in a hospital?" Barney asked. "What will happen to him there?"

"He will rest," Dr. Blauberman said edgily. "I know it must come as a surprise," he said, turning to Leah. "But we must face facts. Mmmm? It will be like going to a good, comfortable, quiet hotel for a few weeks."

"I don't want any hospital!" Mr. Samuels shouted.

"Don't be so old-fashioned, mmmm?" Dr. Blauberman said.

"I don't like the word 'hospital,'" Mr. Samuels said stubbornly.

"There's no proof anywhere that psychoanalysis is scientific," Victor said.

"I know you're a qualified doctor," Leah said. "I looked you up in the medical directory."

Thanks. Dr. Blauberman let out a thick, impatient sigh. Thanks a lot. So what did she want him to do?

"And you belong to the most reliable analytic organization.

177

You wouldn't belong if you weren't a good doctor." She stopped.

How many of these gratuitous progress reports on himself was he supposed to sit here and listen to?

"The doctor sees inside," Leah went on. "The doctor has scientific knowledge."

Thanks an *awful* lot.

"Leah is the expert on all this stuff," Barney said to Dr. Blauberman.

"You went to C.C.N.Y. and to N.Y.U. Medical School," Leah said. "And you interned—"

"Yes, I know," Dr. Blauberman interrupted. This girl seemed to be hypnotizing herself with the recitation of his academic history. Who the hell asked her to bring all that up?

"I want to know about my son!" Mr. Samuels shouted. "I want him to be all right!"

"So you get him to fight society," Dr. Blauberman said quickly. It was all he could do not to give way to the temptation to argue with this ignorant man.

"You mean Pop is no pinochle player?" Vic said, with heavy sarcasm.

"I always liked to stay home and not run around," Mr. Samuels said, in slightly lower tones.

"I'm like that, too," Ephraim said.

"Maybe Dr. Blauberman thinks you act neurotically because who else is still a Socialist?" Leah said to her father.

"Are *you* a Socialist?" Mr. Samuels said to his daughter. "Or Barney? If Vic wants to be a Socialist, he has the right. Or me."

"You told me you voted Democratic," Victor said to his father-in-law.

"So this year *you* are the only Socialist," Mr. Samuels said.

"I didn't mean that," Leah said. "I was trying to explain something that might give Dr. Blauberman the wrong idea about us. Sometimes this family doesn't communicate," she said to Dr. Blauberman.

Dr. Blauberman gave her a friendly "So."

"We communicate more than you think we communicate," Vic said. "We really communicate, so we don't have to waste time telling each other we're communicating."

"All I'm trying to tell Dr. Blauberman," Leah said, "is that nobody else waits forty years to name his son after Eugene Victor Debs. Things like that might give him the wrong idea about us. The point is, Dr. Blauberman, we really *like* the name. Or take how I sit in the playground with the other mothers and listen to them tell about going out. They go to theatre parties. They go to affairs. We don't even attend the P.-T.A. But that doesn't mean—"

"I always say if she wants to go to the P.-T.A., let *her* go to the P.-T.A.," Victor said.

"*I* don't want to go to the P.-T.A.," Leah said.

"I hate the idea of sending my son Jimmy to school at all," Barney said.

"He doesn't mean it," Leah said. "He'll send Jimmy to school."

"I mean, school can kill the spirit of a kid, the way they run most schools. Pop always said it, and it's true," Barney said.

"It's true," Mr. Samuels said, and the rest of the family gave strong signs of being with him all the way.

"If I may be allowed to say something—" Dr. Blauberman began.

"I want Jimmy to be free!" Barney said, as an afterthought, and again the whole family nodded with him.

And Vic had an afterthought, too, which he immediately

179

passed along to Dr. Blauberman. "Those playground mothers!" he said, "*They* communicate. Yakkety-yakkety-yak. My-husband-made-a-million-dollars-yesterday. Yakkety-yak."

"Who's fighting society?" Mr. Samuels said. "Because I don't push Eephie to be aggressive?"

"What for?" Vic said with a scornful laugh. "For what?"

"Dr. Blauberman wants Eephie to be more successful with the clarinet," Leah said. "And Dr. Fifield, too. Dr. Fifield told him he should be getting more out of it."

"Well, my idea of what to get out of it isn't the same as Dr. Blauberman's idea," Ephraim said.

"So maybe you're supposed to have big ambitions, like going on television," Victor said.

"And is that such an unhealthy ambition?" Dr. Blauberman found himself saying, and was surprised that he had actually got a word in.

"Aha! The cat is out of the bag!" Victor said, raising his voice.

"What about having a consultation?" Barney asked. "With Dr. Radelsheim?"

"He's the European doctor Eephie heard about?" Leah said eagerly, and blew her nose.

"European doctor?" Mr. Samuels asked, turning to Ephraim.

"That bassoonist, Charlie," Barney said to Ephraim. "You know, he told you you and Dr. Blauberman ought to have a real consultation with this Dr. Hans Radelsheim?"

"I saw Dr. Radelsheim this morning," Ephraim said. "He's a nice guy."

"Nobody told me about any Dr. Radelsheim!" Mr. Samuels said. "Why didn't you tell me before?"

"Eephie just happened to mention it once," Barney said.

"Charlie was begging Eephie to go to see him," Vic said.

The family discussion was off again. Dr. Blauberman felt himself sinking under Samuelses. Air! Air!

"Charlie is the good-natured, fat one, always making jokes!" Mr. Samuels was saying, with enthusiasm, with excitement.

"The one with the fat wife with freckles on her arms, like Terry's!" Barney said. "Terry is my wife," he said to Dr. Blauberman.

"I am happy to hear that," Dr. Blauberman said.

"Is Charlie the one who played with you at the Y, the Schoenberg?" Leah asked Ephraim.

"Wasn't that wild?" Ephraim said. "And the Mozart Divertimenti."

"You were going to get him started playing jazz," Barney said. "Isn't Charlie the one you were going to make one of the first jazz bassoonists in history?" He laughed.

The whole damn family laughed. Killing themselves laughing on the Doctor's time. Christ!

"Charlie is a wild bassoonist!" Ephraim said. "He plays chamber music with Dr. Radelsheim. Dr. Radelsheim plays the oboe."

"So," Dr. Blauberman said. "The oboe plays with the bassoon. Mmmm?"

The family didn't seem to notice him. "Dr. Radelsheim plays the oboe?" Mr. Samuels was saying with delight.

"He knows a lot about music and about musicians," Ephraim said. "Charlie is crazy about him."

"Charlie!" Dr. Blauberman said. "Is Charlie a bassoonist or a doctor?"

"Thank God he's a bassoonist," Victor said.

"Be quiet!" Mr. Samuels said to Victor. "I want to know—"

181

He turned to Dr. Blauberman. "Could you arrange for a consultation with Dr. Radelsheim?" He asked the question in a quiet, confident tone.

"There's no need for a consultation," Dr. Blauberman said. "Dr. Radelsheim called me, and I discussed Ephraim's case over the telephone. You must realize that doctors talk to each other in a way that they can't possibly discuss the case with the family of a patient. *You* understand, mmmm?" he said specifically to Leah. She nodded.

"You mean you want Eephie to be shoved into a hospital just like that?" Victor said.

"Not shoved," Dr. Blauberman said. "He signs himself in, and he signs himself out. Now, you people don't have so much money you want to throw it away running from one doctor to another, do you? I advise, for Ephraim, rest in a hospital."

"I'm not signing myself into any hospital," Ephraim said to Dr. Blauberman. "You know that. Why are you making such a big issue of it with my family?"

"No hospital," Mr. Samuels said with determination. "He doesn't need a hospital."

"What the hell is the matter with you people?" Dr. Blauberman said.

"Is that how you talk to an older man?" Vic said.

Mr. Samuels blushed. "It doesn't matter," he said. "I am Eephie's father, and I know what he needs."

His pronunciation of "father" grated on Dr. Blauberman's nerves.

"I don't know about psychoanalysis, but I know about my family, and I know about Eephie," Mr. Samuels was saying. "Eephie doesn't need a hospital."

The other members of the family nodded in agreement and

182

looked at him with respect. They seemed to relax in unison. "This is all theoretical, because I'm not *going* to any hospital," Ephraim said.

Dr. Blauberman dropped his pipe on the floor. He felt a surge of rage coming up in him. "I've been Ephraim's doctor for a year," he said. Now *he* was raising *his* voice. But maybe that was just what these thickskulled people needed. Maybe that was something they could understand. "I know Ephraim! I've sat here patiently with you people, trying to give you some professional advice. If you want to disregard it, that is up to you." He paused. "All I can do is warn you."

Ephraim looked scared. "Dr. Radelsheim told me it's important for me to get back to my music," he said.

Dr. Blauberman made impatient noises. Oh, that bigmouth Radelsheim!

"Did you ask Dr. Radelsheim about the sleeping pills?" Mr. Samuels said to Ephraim.

"No, Pop," Ephraim said. "All he said was it was a shame I couldn't sleep, because musicians have to get their sleep."

Leah put her wet wad of Kleenex into her purse and smiled, first at Ephraim and then at Dr. Blauberman.

"Eephie will cut down gradually the way he takes the pills," Mr. Samuels said. "He should never have started with the pills." He no longer sounded angry. He said the last almost apologetically.

"I'll stick with Pop," Ephraim said.

"Pop," Dr. Blauberman found himself saying aloud, as if he were trying the word out. "Pop. Pop." He gave a nervous giggle. So. He wants Pop. Let Pop have him. But Dr. Blauberman felt a curious pang. The father's straw-colored, kinky eyebrows *were*, he noticed, the original model for the boy's.

183

The way his deep lines alongside his mouth were like the lines his father had.

"We'll make out at home," Mr. Samuels said. "What would Eephie do in a hospital?"

"People live in hospitals and die in hospitals, same as anywhere else," Dr. Blauberman said wearily. He saw them all start and look toward their father. Again Dr. Blauberman felt the pang.

"I know what I am doing," Mr. Samuels said. He stood up. Everybody else in the family stood up, too. At last. They were going.

They stood quietly for a moment, looking at him in silence. Then they started out of the office. Dr. Blauberman had meant to stay in his chair, but instead he got up and trailed the family out to the waiting room, expecting them to stop, to say they would do what he had advised. He wanted them to get out of his sight, but he wanted, also, to hold on to them a little longer. "Mr. Samuels—" he said. They all stopped. They all looked around at him. He saw how like old Abe Letkin Ephraim's father was. The same posture. The same inflection. The same. His own father had the inflection, too. But his father was not the same. His father was a cold-blooded son of a bitch. Dr. Blauberman sniffed. "I've given you some serious advice about how to help your son," he said. But he was aware that all the authority had gone out of his voice.

"I know, Doctor," Mr. Samuels said. "You did what you thought was right." He headed for the door and opened it. Dr. Blauberman followed him, and looked at the collie puppy tied to his umbrella stand on the thick salmon-pink carpet. Probably shedding.

Ephraim went over to the puppy and untied him. The puppy began licking his hand.

"Freud loved dogs," Leah said to Dr. Blauberman. "Freud had several chows. He really loved dogs."

"Our old dog, Blackie, who died—you should have seen him, Dr. Blauberman," Mr. Samuels said. "When he died, it broke our hearts. It takes some people a long time to get over a thing like that."

"This collie is a terrific puppy," Ephraim said.

"Touch his head, Doctor," Mr. Samuels said. "Feel how silky he is."

Dr. Blauberman stared at Mr. Samuels, and then at Ephraim, and then at the dog. For a moment, he thought of giving them a real sendoff—of saying "Lotsa luck!" But he didn't. As he swung the door shut on the family, he heard Mr. Samuels say, "Come, children. Let's go home."

★ IX ★

A COUPLE OF MONTHS after Phyllis and Larry Elmendorf had Spencer over to meet Barbara Kirsch, Phyllis telephoned Spencer at his office to say she wanted to come in about her ulcer, and at the same time she invited him out to their place in Connecticut for the weekend. Phyllis suggested that Spencer pick up Barbara Kirsch and her three-year-old daughter, Bunny, and drive them out for the weekend, too. Barbara's husband had been killed in an automobile accident the previous winter, leaving her with Bunny and a six-year-old boy. Barbara's mother was taking the boy for the weekend, Phyllis said; Barbara's mother was a doll. "You two kids need a weekend with us," Phyllis said over the telephone.

She sounded so friendly, her intonation joining him so

warmly to Barbara, that Spencer's heart flipped. He didn't have to stop and think about it at all, he realized; he knew immediately that he really *wanted* to do it. He made a quick note to himself that he was sensing real development, real progress, in himself; this was one decision he did not need to work out first with Dr. Blauberman.

"Bobbie tells me that you two kids have been dat-ing," Phyllis went on, in a singsong.

It was true; they had been dating. Everything was going so easily and so quickly. Soon after he met Barbara at the Elmendorfs', she had called him up and invited him to go to the opening of a Broadway play that Larry Elmendorf had invested in. Spencer just couldn't believe that it was happening to *him*. Ever since then, his mind had seemed to be floating several feet above his body, and he had kept trying to get back into himself, so that he could really take part in what was going on. Spencer was facing his fortieth birthday, and Barbara was a good ten years younger, but Phyllis was putting him back in time, where he felt he belonged, where he had missed his life. He was full of wonder and gratitude, but he was too excited to talk. He felt so many strange, untried sensations that he was unable to utter more than a choked cough.

"I hear you and Bobbie have discovered that you're both rabid liberals—left of the New Frontier," Phyllis said. She had a hoarse voice, which she used loudly, in the manner Spencer had learned belonged to the confident rich. The voice knocked against his eardrum, but Spencer liked it.

"She's a lovely individual," he said.

"So get with it, boy, get with it," Phyllis said, with a rasping laugh. "If you don't mind a little *in loco parentis*-ing push."

187

"Bobbie has very real values, frankly," Spencer said, and gave another nervous cough.

"Wait till you meet Benny, her father," Phyllis said. "Benny's on the right-wing side, part lower-echelon John Loeb, part Uris Brothers, and with a dash of Barry Goldwater. But a real sweet guy. Bobbie got a twenty-five-dollar contribution out of him for Sailboat Seltzer's special study project on 'Psychoanalysis and Negro Integration.'"

"Frankly, she got ten out of me," Spencer said.

Dr. Seltzer had analyzed Phyllis and had been very helpful to Larry, too, Phyllis had told Spencer, and now the Elmendorfs and Dr. Seltzer and his wife, Effie, spent a lot of time together. Dr. Seltzer was very influential in psychoanalytic circles, Spencer knew from Dr. Blauberman, who often referred to Sailboat, in a rather hostile way, Spencer thought, but with admiration, as "a key figure in modern analysis." For one reason or another, Dr. Seltzer had not been able to obtain more than three thousand dollars from a private foundation—only enough to cover a secretary—for his project, so he had gone ahead on his own, with a full-time researcher on salary, as well as nine volunteers, including Phyllis and Bobbie. Phyllis wanted to help Sailboat lead what he described as "the movement to bring Psychic Apparatus closer to everyday American life." To date, Sailboat's project consisted of four separate studies, called "Overdevelopment of Ego Cathexis in Mississippi"; "Racism, Problems of Acting Out in the Pentagon and the White House, and the Superego"; "Color, Job Discrimination, and Pregenitality"; and "Phylogenetic Thrust, Dr. Martin Luther King, Jr., and the Democratic Party."

"Benny thinks that Ego Cathexis is a new listing on the market," Phyllis was saying on the phone. "You'll be mad for Benny."

188

Spencer smiled at the mouthpiece of the telephone and rubbed his eye with his knuckle. This gesture was habitual, and he had discovered, with Dr. Blauberman's help, that it dated back to when he was three years old and that it was connected with his mother's insistence that he keep his knees clean.

"We're going to start the weekend off with a cocktail party —the informal bit," Phyllis was saying. "With only people we like."

"No drinking for *you*, dear," Spencer said, amazed at his own manner with Phyllis, who was not only older than he but much, much richer and more sophisticated. He swallowed the fright he felt at his own authority with her. Though he had not yet told her, he planned to have her operated on for her ulcer very soon. He was sure about the chronic, penetrating ulcer and the damage, but her intractable pain and other symptoms just might indicate several interesting possibilities. He would make tests for all of them, once he had her in the hospital. Long ago, in the days of his interneship, Spencer had discovered that doing a lot of tests made a good impression on patients. After all, if the tests turned out to be negative, Phyllis and Larry wouldn't complain. Like most patients, they would be too busy feeling relief and thankfulness, especially if they had thought there might be something worse than an ulcer.

"I promise to be good," Phyllis said.

Her eagerness to accept his authority added to his sense of fright. He felt scared, actually, every time he called her by her first name. The Elmendorfs were still "new" patients to him. Their former internist had given up his practice after suffering Coronary No. 2, and had, for a compensation, turned over his practice to several younger men. Dick Freisleben, Phyllis's dermatologist, had alerted Spencer, who

189

had taken about three dozen of the patients, all of them well heeled. Larry and Phyllis Elmendorf had hit it off with Spencer from the start, and Spencer had become very fond of them. Both had talked to him about a sexual problem that Spencer had some fine classified information on, thanks to Dr. Blauberman, and Spencer had been able to be very helpful to the Elmendorfs. Consequently, they had opened their Park Avenue apartment and their place in Connecticut to him. They gave a lot of dinner parties, many of them having to do with the good liberal causes, and they invited Spencer to all of them. Spencer couldn't get over the fact that both Elmendorfs were deep-seated liberals, even though Larry was in Wall Street. Yet there wasn't anything seedy or unpleasant about their progressiveness, and everybody they knew seemed to be liberal or rich or attractive or interesting, and sometimes all four at once. It was hard for Spencer to believe, in the light of all this, that the Elmendorfs would be so interested in *him*. Yet Phyllis and Larry both were always asking him to be with them. Slowly, and pushing down the fear that what was happening might at any moment be taken away from him, he began to feel he belonged with them. It made him feel proud.

"They really *need* me," he reported to Dr. Blauberman. "They want me around socially. It reassures them."

"Give and take," Dr. Blauberman replied. "Take and give. Mmmm?"

"I *like* Phyllis," Spencer said. "You'd never guess she had all that money."

"The pool you say they are building in Connecticut," Dr. Blauberman said. "It is a *heated* pool?"

"Heated and constantly changing water," Spencer said. "It cost so much dough it isn't even funny."

"So. Probably they got a special price," Dr. Blauberman said. "He is in chemicals in Wall Street? Chlorine, maybe?"

"You want me to talk about chlorine?" Spencer said, horizontally, and resentfully. At the end of the previous hour, they had been trying to get at the meaning of another aspect of his childhood relationship to his mother—the battles-before-the-kisses—and he wanted Dr. Blauberman to remember that they had been talking about this and ask him to get going again.

To his amazement, instead of remarking upon his hostility, Dr. Blauberman laughed and said, "Everybody likes to have a pool, a heated pool—even a psychoanalyst. Psychoanalysts are human, too. Yes?"

"The other night . . ." Spencer began. The other night, during one of his infrequent visits to his parents, he had been looking at photographs of himself at the wistful, unsmiling, thin-faced age of three. The albums had been dragged out to impress their dinner guests, the Hiram Stones. Mr. Stone had once bought a policy from Spencer's father, who sold life insurance. Spencer had discovered on his arrival—ahead of the Stones, fortunately—that his father planned to urge Mr. Stone to increase the size of his policy. "What makes you think you can get Mr. Stone to add to his coverage?" Spencer told his father. "I notice you've been selling less lately, not more. Don't overdo it. Don't push your luck."

It was a lousy evening. There was forced interest and enthusiasm over the photographs in the albums. Mr. Stone, who still had the rather special condition that required a weekly treatment, which Spencer attended to, on a retainer, repeatedly exclaimed that he never would have recognized Spencer from the albums. "You look anemic," he said, "even in your hair." As a child, Spencer had been blond.

"Spencer had such tiny, gorgeous ears," Spencer's mother said. "He still has them. Very tiny ears for a man."

"That's why he can't hear my troubles," Spencer's father said. Then Mr. Fifield, who had a great repertoire of Borscht Circuit jokes, decided to tell a joke. "Two Jews are going to be shot," he said to Mr. Stone. "So one of the Jews asks for a blindfold. The other Jew turns to him and says, 'Sh-h-h! Don't make trouble!' "

Mr. Stone was not amused. "Being Jewish myself," he said, "I'm entitled to say the Jews never know when they're well off."

Soon after that, Spencer made some excuse about having to go to the hospital and left his parents to entertain the Stones.

Toward the end of the hour, Dr. Blauberman got the discussion back to Larry and Phyllis, and Spencer found himself telling Dr. Blauberman that the Elmendorfs had "a very sound relationship." It was a second marriage for Phyllis; she had a married daughter by her first marriage and no children with Larry.

"The Elmendorfs are good together, even though Phyllis is the one with the original dough," Spencer explained. "Larry used to be her caddie at the country club, but she really fell in love with him anyway."

"But you say that Larry makes money now on the market?" Dr Blauberman said. "He did not use her money for that?"

"Originally," Spencer said. "He's younger than she is, but they're very close. They have everything in common. All the forward-looking interests."

"To them everybody is human?" Dr. Blauberman said.

192

"Mmmm? They are ideal patients. And maybe you are gaining new insight into your patients. Yes?"

"Yes," Spencer said.

After all his years with Dr. Blauberman, Spencer should not have questioned even for a minute that the Doctor had his interests at heart when he asked about the Elmendorfs, and really was concerned about Spencer's medical practice. With the Elmendorfs, at last, his life was on the right track. Now he didn't have to bother—as he had for years and years —with trying to reach out to patients who offered him nothing but their own neurotic fears and dependencies, and never paid their bills on time, and always seemed to wind up throwing a barrage of confusing feelings at him, feelings he could never comprehend. He had always been so baffled by patients who seemed to be pulling at him, trying to get something out of him that he couldn't give, and so made him feel that he had failed them. With patients like the Elmendorfs, everything was clear, simple, and, as Dr. Blauberman said, rewarding.

Now the Elmendorfs were rewarding him with Barbara Kirsch and her children. A few days after bringing Barbara and him together, the Elmendorfs had given another of their inimitable dinner parties, and Barbara had been seated next to Spencer. On his other side Phyllis had placed Mrs. Bertha Cornwall Durlingham-Smith, the famous Negro psychiatric social worker.

"The Elmendorfs are up on the latest," Spencer had reported to Dr. Blauberman. "They're deeply involved in the Negro question, and they really *work* at it."

Across the table at the dinner party were Sailboat Seltzer and Effie. And Barbara was perfect. For one thing, she knew the Seltzers very well and was very casual with them, taking over for Spencer, who felt so shaky in the analyst's presence that he couldn't look him in the eye. In his nervousness, Spencer started talking about his own analysis, and Barbara smoothly switched the conversation to some minor point in *her* own analysis, and got Spencer off the hook. Barbara was so damn poised. Over the Baked Alaska, Spencer got into a terrific discussion with Mrs. Durlingham-Smith about the recent increase in V.D. cases, mostly Negroes, being treated in the hospital clinic, and Barbara contributed a lot to the discussion. Afterward, over brandy, Phyllis took Spencer and Barbara aside and asked, "How did you two kids get on with Bertie Smith?"

"Frankly, she's a very real person," Spencer said. "I've got to hand it to you."

"We just like each other," Phyllis said. "Larry and I only invite people we like."

"Bertie knew more about syphilis than I do, frankly," Spencer said. "And this young lady"—he grabbed Barbara at the back of the neck—"knows a lot about it, too."

"I did a paper about it at Barnard," Barbara said. "And I've got the kind of mind, facts always stick."

"I'm that way, too, actually," Spencer said.

"Bertie is a gem," Phyllis said. "We'll all do it again soon."

That night, when Spencer took Barbara home, he told her all about his Cousin Bonnie in Bridgeport, who had won a beauty contest a couple of years before as Miss Brass Hardware of that city, and how Cousin Bonnie had known a wonderful Negro boy in high school, very handsome, an honor student and captain of the football team, who was "very clean-cut." The boy had asked Bonnie to go to a school dance with him, precipitating a family crisis. Bonnie's mother had put the kibosh on the date. So Bonnie had gone to the dance

194

with another boy, but she had *danced* with the Negro boy twice. "It took a lot of guts," Spencer said to Barbara.

"Phyllis has guts," Barbara said. "It took guts to marry Larry. He was just this poor, ordinary Jewish boy."

In a vague way, Spencer felt he was being complimented. "One thing I don't completely understand—maybe you can help me," he said. "Is Dr. Seltzer supposed to socialize with Phyllis? As her analyst, I mean?"

"She's finished," Barbara said. "It's all right to socialize now."

Spencer had found, more and more, that he could really depend on Barbara for guidance and help. She knew as many answers as Dr. Blauberman. Every morning, when he arrived for his analytic hour, Dr. Blauberman greeted him with a smile and made no secret of the fact that he was pleased with the changes in Spencer's life. Dr. Blauberman had entirely dropped his program of spurring Spencer on to make love objects of various other young women. It had got so that Dr. Blauberman started every session off with inquiries about the Elmendorfs and Bobbie Kirsch.

"It's all opening up now, Dr. Blauberman," Spencer would say.

"Basically," Dr. Blauberman would say, cheering him on, "you have all the makings of an ordinary, conventional, normal person."

Most wonderful of all, Spencer actually began to *feel* different. All his senses were heightened. He thought he could see so much more. He thought he could hear more. He even thought he could feel.

"So," Phyllis said, by way of concluding the telephone conversation, "you drive Bobbie out in time for the party?"

"Will do," Spencer said. "Will do."

Looking forward to Friday afternoon, Spencer felt a special kind of exhilaration, and it didn't turn out to be momentary. It stayed with him. The next morning, at the start of his analytic hour, when he told Dr. Blauberman about the coming weekend, the analyst was all approval.

"Phyllis says that Larry is bringing an investment specialist up for the weekend who will give me some advice on buying stocks," Spencer said.

Dr. Blauberman said, in a kidding tone, that he wished he could go along.

"You know, Bobbie is getting very interested in *you*," Spencer said. "She keeps asking me. She wants to know everything. I think I feel a little jealous."

"So," Dr. Blauberman said. "Bobbie transfers to *me* now. Mmmm?"

"I think I'm *jealous*," Spencer said.

"The Elmendorfs—they ask about me, too?" Dr. Blauberman inquired, and Spencer said of course, the Elmendorfs always asked about him, too.

"They must have a big place, the Elmendorfs, to hold so many guests," Dr. Blauberman said. "No?"

"Fourteen rooms and a guesthouse sleeping six," Spencer said. "The guesthouse has these double-decker beds. The whole motif is nautical. Reminds me of my days in the Navy."

"Forget associating!" Dr. Blauberman said sternly. "You go for a fun weekend. Forget the analysis, mmmm?"

"Funny about 'Bobbie' and 'Bunny' and 'Benny'—they sound so much like my Cousin Bonnie," Spencer said. "And my mother is 'Beattie'."

"Forget associating, I said! We do not bring up any of that material today."

"Phyllis is crazy about Bobbie," Spencer said. "Phyllis says

196

that Bobbie won't take any foolishness—that Bobbie knows how to lay down the law, you know? Phyllis says I need that."

Dr. Blauberman said nothing.

"She gives me a feeling of security, something to hold on to," Spencer said.

"Phyllis?"

"Bobbie," Spencer said.

"The investment man Larry is bringing," Dr. Blauberman said. "He will give you market tips?"

"Frankly, I really *feel* like making a lot of money now," Spencer said. "After all, Phyllis and Larry do good things with their money. I mean, they give to all the good causes. All the latest movements that are important. They're not defensive about their money, like some rich people, who act as though you're always trying to get some of it. I want to make money for Bobbie. I really do. It's a healthy sign, isn't it?"

"Forget about healthy. What is healthy?" Dr. Blauberman said. "Take the market tips. And forget about healthy. Forget about the analysis. Until after the weekend."

Spencer left the couch in a state of bliss.

Phyllis had arranged her visit to Spencer's office for just before lunch, and, after he had examined her, Spencer took her to the Kwik Kitchen around the corner from his office for a bite. He wanted to avoid telling her about going into the hospital for tests until after the weekend, and this wasn't difficult. They both, it turned out, wanted to talk about Bobbie. Phyllis had almost finished a pastrami sandwich before Spencer noticed what she was eating. She was talking about a beautiful little piece of property that Bobbie liked that was next to the Elmendorfs' place in Connecticut. Larry could get the property for Spencer for hardly anything.

197

"It has a nice little house," Phyllis was saying. "Nothing special, but functional. And you'll be spending most of your time at our place anyway— Dammit, Spencer, I've got this rotten, gnawing pain!" She clutched at her midriff with her left hand, and the pastrami sandwich, in her other hand, was right in front of Spencer's face, and that was how he happened to notice it.

"Naughty," Spencer said decisively, and took the sandwich out of her hand and set it on the plate.

He saw for the first time, after all the months he had been looking at her, that Phyllis had a mole over her left eyebrow. She wore a large diamond-and-emerald turtle pin on the lapel of her lavender silk suit; the turtle's head emerged from the diamond-studded shell with two rubies for eyes.

"It can't be from the pastrami," Phyllis said. "That takes an hour before you feel it."

And suddenly he realized that she was looking at him like any other patient in trouble. He felt wonderful.

"Let's find out what in Christ's name is going on with my whatsis and get it over with," Phyllis said.

Spencer lit a cigarette. "We'll get the picture on your whatsis soon," he said.

"What do I have to do first?" Phyllis said.

"Leave everything to me," Spencer said.

"I want you to get rid of this damn pain for me," Phyllis said. "I want to stick around. Promise me?"

"I promise you," Spencer said. "You'll dance at my wedding."

Friday started with a hilarious hour and a half in the operating room. As an attending physician on the staff of the hospital, Spencer was in charge of a medical ward, and one of the ward patients was being operated on for gallstones. Spencer stood by with Max Pooley, who was operating. The patient was a husky young man who had a tattoo in four colors across his stomach. The tattoo showed a large heart enclosing the words "True Love. Mom. Dad. Lucy." Pooley was about to start cutting on the "Mom," but Spencer stopped him. Spencer was feeling more at ease with Pooley than he could ever remember. It just wasn't right, he told Pooley, to start by cutting "Mom." One of the young surgical residents giggled so violently that a nurse had to help him change his mask. "Why not start with 'Lucy'?" Spencer said.

"All right, why not?" Pooley said. "I can afford to be charitable. I just won the Metrecal Award. The No-Belly Prize."

Everybody was laughing so hard it was a wonder that Pooley could hold the knife steady, Spencer thought. But, of course, he did. He was a marvel, that Pooley. A genius. He really knew how to cut. Afterward, while they were washing up, Pooley told Spencer that he had promised to take a couple of his grandchildren to California, to visit Disneyland, during Christmas week. Now it seemed to Spencer that he was seeing Pooley for the first time, too. Pooley's pince-nez and bushy white hair gave him such an elegant, elder-statesman appearance.

"I'm playing Papa this weekend," Spencer said. "Taking a friend and her three-year-old out to the country." He helped himself to a few of the paper containers from the O.R. "Insurance," he said, winking at Pooley. "You know the way kids get. In a car."

From the O.R., Spencer made it downstairs to Private a few minutes too late to see the Davidson boy out of this world.

"We tried to page you, but he went out too fast," the resident told Spencer.

The parents of the boy stared at Spencer, stunned. Spencer

199

had spent a lot of time with them, preparing them for the fact that their son would never leave the hospital alive. He had had dinner with them twice a week for the past ten weeks. It was amazing, Spencer had told Dr. Blauberman, how the parents plied him with questions about their son's illness. "They're overcompensating because of guilt feelings," Spencer said, and was congratulated on his insight into the situation.

Mrs. Davidson held a gift—a white handkerchief box tied with a blue silk ribbon. "We got it for you last night, to give to your girl friend, maybe," she said. "Because we took you away from her so much."

Spencer got loose from the Davidsons as fast as possible. He decided not to look in on Rod Miller. Rod had a persistent infection in a broken leg. As a boy, Spencer had gone to camp with Rod, who was now an English teacher. Until a month or so ago, Spencer had given a lot of time to Rod and his wife, but now he found Rod just too burdensome.

"Poor Rod," Spencer said to Barbara once, when they were discussing the patients he had in the hospital. "He just resumed psychoanalysis, and he's scared stiff people at his school will find out. He made me promise to keep it confidential."

"You can tell *me*," Barbara said.

"He's such a downbeat character," Spencer said. "He just found out his wife can't have any children."

"Poor Rod," Barbara said.

Luckily, the door to Rod's room was closed, so he wouldn't know Spencer had been in that day without stopping to see him.

In his office, Spencer saw about ten patients. He brushed them off crisply when they started talking about matters not directly related to the business at hand. He was especially abrupt with Mrs. Stone, who started her usual routine with him of asking whether he knew this doctor and that. She always had two or three new names to ask about. Although Spencer ordinarily liked to gossip with Mrs. Stone, today he said coldly, "I haven't heard of them, frankly. I have to go now," he added, ushering her out. Mrs. Stone would just have to adjust. Her husband ran the show, and Spencer was not afraid of anything that Mrs. Stone might do.

The only patient Spencer gave a little extra time to was Pete Himmel, who was on a weekend in town from college. He was in his first year. He had a number of questions he wanted to ask about sex. Spencer was touched by Pete's innocence, his complete faith in Spencer, and his automatic assumption that Spencer knew all the answers. In particular, Pete wanted to know whether it was all right to go up to a certain establishment with a reputation for kindness to college boys.

"Go ahead, don't worry about it," Spencer said, feeling very paternal and protective. "Someday you'll have a real relationship with a woman, but in the meantime, frankly, we all have our physical needs."

"I can really *talk* to you," Pete said. "You really understand."

"The thing to remember," Spencer said, speaking the words that Dr. Blauberman had taught him, "is don't feel guilty about anything that happens."

Spencer was still exhilarated on the drive up to Connecticut with Bobbie alongside him and Bunny stretched out on the shelf above the back seat, under the rear window, asleep. After reaching the Merritt Parkway, Spencer stopped to get some gas. The attendant cleaned the front window and then told Spencer that he would skip the rear one. "I might wake up your little girl," he said. Spencer was delirious, and gave the man a fifty-cent tip. Driving in the heavy traffic, he absent-mindedly turned out of his lane without looking behind him. Another driver had to swerve away from Spencer to avoid hitting him, and shouted an insult. Spencer laughed. He felt like laughing at everything. Bobbie said she had brought along a new pair of slacks, and he laughed at *that*. With this strong, confident, good-looking, dependable girl next to him, he felt his head pounding as he drove. He was *sure* she was good-looking. If he had ever wanted anything at all in his whole life, he wanted Bobbie and everything she had to offer. She was perfect wife material. And patients would be crazy about her, too. That is, his new type of patient—not those screwballs, of both sexes, who had given him so much trouble in the past. If somebody very sick called up and got Bobbie, he knew she wouldn't be thrown by it; she wasn't the type to get upset. She never tired of hearing the medical details of his day. She wanted to know everything about how the Davidson boy went out, and Spencer told her.

"Frankly, it was rough," he said. "I spent a lot of time with his parents that I might have spent with you."

"I had a feeling it would happen today," Bobbie said.

"Patient Griselda," Spencer said to her, and with one hand he took the handkerchief box from the rear of the car and handed it to her. "Open it, Patient Griselda," he said. "Mrs. Davidson said it's for you."

Bobbie untied the blue silk ribbon and opened the box. Inside was a white lace handkerchief with a blue lace border. "It's beautiful," she said, and put the handkerchief in her purse.

"The Davidsons have good taste," Spencer said.

They talked about other patients as they drove, and Spencer told her of the particular service he performed for Mr. Stone each week. "But I think I'm growing away from that," Spencer said. "After all, he doesn't really need a doctor to do that. Anybody can do that for him. It's just that he feels confidence in me." Spencer rubbed his eye. "I worry about taking all that money from him for it."

"You need it more than he does," Bobbie said. He smiled at her. She lit a cigarette. "You think too much," she said, and exhaled a stream of smoke at him. "Every time you start to intellectualize, stop. Don't think. *Feel.*"

It was amazing the way she put her finger on things. He confided to her how he had skipped looking in on Rod Miller that morning. "I feel so sorry for guys like Rod, whose desire for normalcy is constantly being frustrated," he said.

"Remind me to show the handkerchief to Phyllis," Bobbie said.

They then discussed Phyllis's ulcer, and he said he wanted to lure her into the hospital for tests.

"Tell her what you want to do and why," Bobbie said. "Phyllis can take it. She has guts."

"I really *care* what happens to Phyllis," Spencer said.

"Identifying with her husband, hmmm?" Bobbie said.

"I've gained a lot of insight into love relationships," Spencer said.

Under the rear window, Bunny mumbled something in her sleep. Spencer glanced back at the child and told Bobbie he thought Bunny looked like little Caroline Kennedy. And Bobbie, he suddenly realized, had her hair combed just like Jackie's. My God, he thought, here I am, identifying with

203

the President of the United States. For the first time in his life, he was sure he was happy.

Phyllis Elmendorf came up to them as soon as they arrived. The cocktail party was going strong in the patio, with most of the people dressed casually; the men as well as the women were in Bermuda shorts.

"Don't take the time to change now, Spencer," Phyllis said, putting her arm through his. "Bobbie will put Bunny to bed upstairs. I want you down here."

"Pucci?" Spencer said, looking at Phyllis's gold gauzy-silk slacks and matching jacket, both stamped with large butterflies and grasshoppers in green and purple. The ruby-eyed diamond-studded turtle now squatted on her collar.

"Pucci," Phyllis said, looking pleased. "Had this set made in Hong Kong, actually. The two days we spent there on our world tour. They copied my aquamarine Puccis overnight. For about two dollars and fifty cents." She introduced him to a number of people. He wished that Bobbie had stayed with him for support. He felt lost. As Phyllis led him quickly from one young-middle-aged couple to another, he catalogued the impressive jewels—impressive but in good taste —pinned, like Phyllis's turtle, on Pucci shirts and cashmere sweaters with white mink collars. Everybody smiled friendship at Spencer. Then Phyllis left him in order to greet someone else.

An upright piano, painted in red enamel, had been moved out to a corner of the patio, but no one was playing. A young Negro butler held a tray of Martinis-with-lemon-peel out to Spencer. He took one. A Negro maid, with a stiff little white cap on her head and a tiny white apron over a black uniform, stood holding a bowl of shrimp dip in one hand and, in the other, a bowl of giant potato chips. Spencer took a potato chip and scooped up some of the shrimp paste.

"Spence! Long time no see!" It was Dick Freisleben. He was in training on the side to become a full-time psychoanalyst, but Spencer thought he ought to stick to dermatology. Freisleben went around these days acting as though he were in on special secrets and had some official right to be euphoric. He was also in the process of divorcing his wife. "Isn't this great?" Freisleben said, looking around with Martini-inspired enthusiasm. "What a joint! Some layout, no, Spence? Here, meet Sophie. Soph is a candidate in training with me." Sophie, a small, stocky woman wearing floral-print shorts, disengaged herself from the shrimp dip and nodded at Spencer. "Soph is working with Sailboat on the big project!" Freisleben went on. "You seen Sailboat yet, Spence?"

There was something irritating about the way Freisleben was so relaxed, so at home with everybody. Spencer doubted if Freisleben *really* addressed Dr. Seltzer by the nickname. He looked around for Barbara.

"Sailboat!" Freisleben called out. "Stranger! Long time no see!"

"Dick!" Sailboat said. "Sophie!" Then he noticed Spencer and said, "Hi there."

"Spencer Fifield," Spencer said, feeling very uncomfortable. "I was just going to look for Bobbie."

Effie came along and said that they were getting up a sailing party to leave at eight in the morning. "Bobbie wants to go," she said to Spencer.

"In that case . . ." Spencer said. For the first time, he was able to look straight into Sailboat's eyes, and now Sailboat also smiled on Spencer.

"It's a deal," Effie said.

205

"Not us!" Freisleben shouted, patting Sophie on the floral-print shorts. "We got various things to do to report back on to our analysts Monday morning." He and Sophie both went for more shrimp dip.

"Isn't Phyllis *some*thing?" Effie said to Spencer. "Who else in Fairfield County would have the nerve to invite a Negro up for the weekend?"

"Where?" Spencer said.

Sailboat tilted his Martini in the direction of a very handsome young man with light-brown skin. He was wearing tartan-plaid wool Bermuda shorts and a camel's-hair jacket with gold buttons, and he had just sat down at the upright piano. Several of the guests began edging over toward him. Just then, Larry Elmendorf joined Spencer and the Seltzers. In one hand Larry was carrying an ashtray, and in the other a highball. A lady's coat was slung over one shoulder. There was still a touch of the caddie about Larry Elmendorf. Although he had a rather obtrusive potbelly and was almost completely bald except for a few wisps of hair at the base of his skull, he had the freckled face of a barefoot boy on a calendar going fishing down a sunlit country road. Bowing pleasantly to everybody, he managed to crook the arm holding the ashtray around Spencer's shoulders in greeting. Not since the days when his maternal grandfather was alive had Spencer felt so favored. His grandparents had lived with his father and mother—or, rather, the Fifields and Spencer had lived with the grandparents, in the grandparents' town house —for the first seventeen years of Spencer's life. Only last spring, Spencer had devoted half a dozen sessions with Dr. Blauberman to his grandfather. "Grandpa *liked* me" was the way Spencer summed up what he had learned at the end of the sessions. Larry Elmendorf liked him, too. He kept his arm

206

around Spencer, hanging on while swaying back and forth gently in conversation with the Seltzers.

"Shet mah mouth, Larry, you trying to get the K.K.K. to crash this wingding?" Sailboat said. "I've got to hand it to you."

"You're wonderful," Effie said. "Larry, you and Phyllis are wonderful."

"You mean Johnny?" Larry said, indicating the young man at the piano. "We only invite people we like. I know Johnny's big brother, Tom. Tom is the most influential broker in Harlem. You'd be surprised what the weekly figure is of what they buy up there in Harlem."

"Wouldn't surprise me," Sailboat said. "Not after our study on the Phylogenetic Thrust."

"The middle-class Negro has drive," Spencer said. "I have a Negro patient, a lawyer, and the suppressed hostility—"

But Larry, his arm still crooked around Spencer, wasn't paying attention. Neither was anybody else, and Spencer dropped what he was trying to say and looked around for Bobbie.

"Tom sent Johnny over to me to see if there's anything I can do for the kid," Larry was saying to Sailboat Seltzer. "Seems the kid gets into trouble. Overshadowed by successful powerhouse older brother—that sort of thing, you know?"

"I try not to work on weekends," Sailboat said.

Larry laughed. "The kid got thrown out of Harvard," he said. "Drank, and flunked out, you know?"

"He probably needs help," Spencer said.

"I need a refill," Sailboat said, turning the stem of his empty Martini glass. "Where's that butler of yours?"

There was a rumor around that Sailboat had gone sailing earlier in the summer with the Kennedys at Hyannis Port. Sail-

207

boat hadn't exactly quashed the rumor. Dr. Blauberman had found out, however, that Sailboat had indeed visited Hyannis Port, but only to see an actress patient of his who was playing in the Cape Cod Melody Tent. "Dr. Seltzer is a brilliant doctor, but he gets ahead of himself," Dr. Blauberman had told Spencer.

"This patio reminds me of my grandfather's house," Spencer now said. "My grandfather had a town house in the city, with a patio just like this one in the back. A town house is the only way to live in the city." Sailboat owned a town house, where he both lived and kept his office. The house was also the headquarters of the study project on "Psychoanalysis and Negro Integration." He ought to have been interested in the subject of town houses, but apparently he didn't feel like discussing it with Spencer. Larry, however, said, "Nice," and gave Spencer a friendly hug. "Our investment buddy with the hot tips we want will be along later," he said. "I'll get you a drink, Sailboat."

Dick Freisleben came back with Sophie. "Sailboat!" he shouted. "You'll love this! Tell him, Soph!"

"The latest on why people in Great Neck aren't building any fallout shelters," Sophie said.

"This'll kill you!" Freisleben shouted.

"Because they figure they won't *need* them," Sophie said. "They figure if war comes the men will all be at their offices in New York, the women will all be out shopping, the kids will be in school. So why build? For the *help?*"

Everybody laughed the same kind of laugh, united and exact, a laugh that was divided clearly into two parts, two syllables—an "ah" that went uphill quickly into a knowing "hah."

"Isn't that wild?" Freisleben shouted joyously. He used to live, with his about-to-be-divorced wife, in Great Neck.

"I hear Kim Novak is building a fallout shelter," Sailboat said. "They're big in California."

"Frankly, don't you find Kim Novak a very superficial individual?" Spencer said, but again his remark got lost. He began to droop. He noticed it immediately. It was frightening. If only Bobbie would come.

"Where's that drink?" Sailboat said, turning away, and found himself face to face with a Japanese floor lamp. "Don't scare me like that," Sailboat said to the lamp.

Spencer heard exuberant laughter coming from some people standing at the piano. He glanced around. The Negro maid was between the piano and him. There was a particularly blank expression on her face as she stood looking toward the young man at the piano and extending the bowls of shrimp dip and potato chips to Spencer. He took a potato chip, and scooped it into the mixture. Then he nodded in the direction of the piano and said, "Johnny going to start playing now?"

"I don't know, sir," the maid said.

"I mean, did Johnny play before?" Spencer said. "Frankly, I just got here."

"I don't know, sir," the maid repeated.

Spencer put the potato chip down on a table and looked desperately toward the stairway, which he could see through the French doors that opened into the patio. Possibly he should run upstairs and *find* Bobbie—give her a hand, maybe, with Bunny. He tried to focus on the faces of people he had been introduced to a few minutes before. He tried to remember their names, but he couldn't. As he was pushing his way through the crush toward the stairway, he suddenly encountered Phyllis.

"Kitty Lenz, Dr. Spencer Fifield," Phyllis was saying, and

he realized that she was introducing him to a young woman who was wearing tight, fuchsia-colored toreador pants.

Kitty Lenz gave Spencer her hand to shake. It was cold. She looked ill at ease and alone. She kept wetting her lips. Her white lace overblouse fell a couple of inches short of the top of the toreador pants, exposing a smooth, tanned strip of skin. She wore high-heeled gold sandals, her face was heavily made up, and she had long fingernails painted to match the color of her pants. She presented Spencer with an expression of gaiety—an expression that she had probably taken to many other cocktail parties where she had wandered ill at ease and alone. Spencer recognized the expression. In the past, at other parties, he had often found himself drawn to women like her.

"Did you see Bobbie?" Spencer said to Phyllis. "Will Bobbie be down soon?"

"Soon as she gets Bunny to bed," Phyllis said.

"What a trip!" Spencer said expansively. "I expected Bunny to oops in the car, but she slept practically all the way."

"Keep the windows of the car open," Kitty Lenz said. "Don't let them know you're worrying about it, and just don't make a big production out of it. Cute kid at the piano there. I like his gold buttons. Who brought the cute kid at the piano, Phyl?"

"She's three," Spencer said. "And she looks exactly like little Caroline Kennedy." Turning to Phyllis, he said, "I'd better run upstairs and see if I can help Bobbie."

"You stay right here with us, darling," Phyllis said, leaning against him. And then, answering Kitty Lenz, she said, "Johnny's brother is one of our favorite people. Larry does a lot of business with him."

"Such cute buttons," Kitty Lenz said, and gave Spencer a smile.

"Johnny's brother that investment man?" Spencer said.

Phyllis let out a shriek of laughter. "No, darling," she said. "Johnny's brother is relatively small potatoes. We've got something special lined up for you."

"What's up, Doc?" Kitty Lenz said, trying to make herself sound comical. "You need a new stethoscope?"

Phyllis gave another shriek, which was echoed by a burst of laughter from the vicinity of the piano. Spencer saw Sailboat Seltzer pumping Johnny's hand. "My tan is better than your tan!" he said jovially to the young Negro.

Johnny took a newly lighted cigarette out of his mouth and threw back his head and laughed. He laughed for an unusually long time. Everybody around the piano tried to laugh along with him. Then Larry held out his ashtray to Johnny, who snapped the whole cigarette into the tray, scattering sparks on the front of Larry's shirt. Larry picked up the cigarette and put it out, and Johnny threw back his head again and laughed some more.

"Play something, Johnny!" Phyllis called out. Larry saw her and came over, and she gave him a wifely peck on the cheek.

"Johnny sure is adorable," Kitty Lenz said, as though speaking to herself, but looking wistfully at Spencer. "That lad has got beautiful choppers."

Spencer looked away from her without answering.

"Pul-lay som-a-thing!" Phyllis called out to Johnny.

"Does he play?" Larry asked. "I didn't know he played."

"He *must* play," Phyllis said.

"Why?" Kitty Lenz said.

Spencer edged away from her. She was making him feel

nervous. He wanted to stand with Phyllis and Larry without being disturbed by this oddball-screwball.

"How about some Cole Porter, man?" Sailboat said. " 'Night and Day.' How about 'Night and Day'?" Sailboat motioned with his drink to the Elmendorfs to come over to the piano. Spencer started to go with them, but Kitty Lenz held him back by saying quickly, "Dr. Fifield—or am I expected to call you by your first name?"

"Spencer," he said formally.

"Relax, Spencer, I'm harmless. Do you mind if I ask what kind of doctor are you?"

"An internist," Spencer said.

"My ex-husband was an internist. My ex-husband moved out to the Coast. He had this theory that all his patients needed him to mother them—that he was their mother figure. That was his theory. So we got divorced. Maybe you knew him—Dr. Donald Lenz. *Summa cum laude,* Harvard, 1940. Harvard Med School, 1944. His office was on Seventy-third and Park."

"I'd better go up and get Bobbie," Spencer said, but he couldn't move.

On the other side of the piano, Phyllis was asking Johnny to play some Twist music. "Play Chubby Checker," she said.

"How about Joey Dee?" Johnny said softly, and he put his head back and laughed.

"Twist, Johnny!" Phyllis yelled.

"Ray Charles's 'Do the Twist' is better than any of Chubby Checker, frankly," Spencer said.

"What do you know, a Ray Charles man!" Kitty Lenz said. There was something in her tone that Spencer heard as mockery. He lit a cigarette, and he saw his hands were trembling. He felt an old panic. Then, inhaling deeply, he forced himself to concentrate on what he had to remember: He was

212

over the hump now. Dr. Blauberman had led him to his graduation from the lame-duck school of the Kitty Lenzes. He
had graduated from the Rod Millers. He had now reached
what Dr. Blauberman had assured him was the adult level of
the Elmendorfs, of Bobbie Kirsch. He was one of them now.
He had finally joined what Dr. Blauberman liked to call the
human race. And Dr. Blauberman had shown him how to
fight for his position.

"You wear too much makeup," he heard himself say to
Kitty Lenz. She gave him a look of astonishment. He left her
and went over to Larry and Phyllis.

"Cole Porter," Sailboat was saying to Johnny. " 'Night and
Day.' "

Johnny started banging meaninglessly on the piano keys.
Then he lifted his hands high above the keyboard and held
them poised there, and burst into a laugh. The audience began laughing, too.

"Yeah, man!" Sailboat said, and, reaching across a couple
of guests, he took a fresh drink from the Negro butler.

" 'Night and day . . .' " Johnny began, in a high, strained
voice, and he brought both hands, fingers spread out, down
at random, without playing real chords. " 'Night and day . . .
day and night . . . night and day . . .' " He seemed to sing in
bits and pieces of the accepted styles of several popular singers. Then he lifted his head way up high, closed his eyes, and
brought his head way down low, until his chin practically
rested on the keyboard.

Kitty Lenz joined the group at the piano. "He doesn't
know the song, Phyl," she said to Phyllis, but Phyllis had her
eyes closed, and was busy nodding and tapping her foot.

"He's not playing the piano," Kitty Lenz said, touching
Phyllis on the arm. "He's just hitting the keys."

Phyllis opened her eyes, but looked at Sailboat, who was

slapping the side of the piano drunkenly. "Cool, man, cool!" Sailboat said, to the piano.

"'You are the one . . .'" Effie Seltzer put in, lifting her head as Johnny was doing and closing *her* eyes, too.

"'You are the one . . . you are the one . . . you are the one . . .'" Johnny repeated, and struck a few more would-be chords, at opposite ends of the keyboard.

"Why don't you all leave him alone?" Kitty Lenz said, to no one in particular. "He's not playing the piano. There's nothing there. Stop pushing him."

Phyllis gave her a look of annoyance and joined Sailboat in a slapping duet on the wood of the piano. Kitty Lenz was right, Spencer realized. Johnny wasn't really singing, and he wasn't really playing the piano. Spencer looked at Phyllis and Larry and the Seltzers. All four of them now were nodding and foot-tapping a would-be beat to the nonexistent rhythm, the nonexistent melody, the abortive lyrics. Spencer looked back at Kitty Lenz blankly. She could *afford* to stand around telling the truth. She was on the outside of everything anyway.

Just then, Bobbie came into the room. Spencer signalled to her to work her way in alongside him. "How's Bunny?" he said to her, in a loud voice. He took hold of the back of Bobbie's neck and looked over at Kitty Lenz.

"She's fast asleep," Bobbie said.

"Martini, dear?" Spencer said.

"With lemon peel," Bobbie said.

As Spencer headed for the butler and the drinks, he passed Phyllis, who was still tapping her foot enthusiastically, going through all the motions of keeping time, or what she thought was time, to the nonexistent music. For a moment, Spencer felt his panic returning, but then he saw clearly that it didn't matter whether Johnny was playing music or not; the important thing was that everybody *acted* as if he was. Who needed Kitty Lenz?

"Cool?" Phyllis said, smiling at Spencer, smiling at Bobbie, smiling at Johnny at the piano.

"Real cool," Spencer said.

★ X ★

"I forgot to tell you," Lou, the manager of the Freeplace, said to Annie. "Spencer was in here looking for you on your day off."

Annie was filling a sugar container. She misjudged the capacity and spilled some sugar on the table.

"He bent my ear for an hour," Lou said as Annie wiped the tabletop clean with a dishrag. "He was telling me all about the various diseases of his patients. By the time he left, I felt real lousy, like *I* had everything, you know?"

"I'm surprised he was here," Annie said. "I haven't seen him in about three months."

The door of the coffeehouse opened, letting in a blast of cold air from outside. Annie looked up, startled, expecting

216

to see Spencer. With relief, she saw that the newcomer was an actor from one of the Off Broadway plays around the corner.

"Well, anyway, he said he'll probably be in again tonight," Lou said, and went off to change the record on the classical jukebox. For the past half hour, it had been shaking out a repeated stereophonic rendition of the Pianoforte Sonatina by Bartók.

Annie took the actor's order and an order from a bunch of girls who belonged to a guitar club and had their guitars with them, making it necessary for Annie to do a lot of fancy footwork. Annie laughed as she stepped over the guitars. A couple of hours more and her shift would end, and she would go over to the Zero Inn and wait for Josh to take her home. Tonight, Annie wanted to get there in time to hear the trio play "Kind Regards." Josh had composed the number, for her, a couple of weeks ago. On Valentine's Day he had given her an actual old-time valentine he had found in a bookshop; it had a border of paper lace around an oval made of tiny sprigs of green paper fern and a tiny cluster of red paper roses. In the center of the oval was a miniature book open to the words "I send kind regards and hope that you may with pleasure remember in future this day." That had been the inspiration for "Kind Regards." These days, she found herself humming the song constantly. All she wanted at the moment was to go on minding her humming. At best, Spencer was an intrusion.

Every time the door opened, Annie turned toward it uneasily, and after a while there was Spencer, arriving with the same old intimate manner, acting as though he had last seen her that morning at breakfast. One thing about him, however, was different. His usually disorganized face was pulled together in a way that she hadn't seen it for several years.

Spencer sat down at a table and ordered a salami-and-onion sandwich. Annie went out to the kitchen, and by the time she returned with the sandwich, Spencer was acting jumpy. He grabbed a saltcellar and slid it back and forth over the top of the table, talking rapidly, saying he had been working very hard and making a lot of money.

"I really *want* to make a lot of money now," he said mysteriously.

"Nice," Annie said, trying to avoid involvement.

"I mean, I really *care* now," Spencer said.

Annie stood at the table, suddenly trying to recall the melody of "Kind Regards" while she said, "Anything to drink?"

"Chocolate malted," Spencer said.

She left him again, and when she returned with the malted, she sat down at the table with him.

"Frankly, it's time I started making some real money," Spencer said rapidly. He ate nervously. Then he lit a cigarette, dropping it immediately on his new J. Press tweed suit. He slapped at himself to put out the sparks. Order restored, he lit another cigarette. "Frankly, I came here to discuss something with you," he said.

Annie felt a sudden fright. She remembered that her brother Mike had mentioned getting a checkup from Spencer a few weeks before, and thought that Spencer was bringing her bad news about Mike.

"I wanted to tell you myself before you heard it from somebody else," Spencer said.

"Is it Mike?" she asked.

He was avoiding looking at her, and he gave a nervous

little giggle. "Dr. Blauberman said I have to tell you my-self," he said stiffly. "I'm going to get married."

"God, Spencer, you scared me!" she said. "But that's won-derful. Terrifico."

"I know how you must feel," Spencer said, in the same stiff way. "Frankly, that's why Dr. Blauberman insisted that I had to tell you myself."

She stared at him in surprise. "But that's *wonderful,* Spen-cer. It's just that you scared me. I thought you were going to tell me something terrible about Mike." She leaned back in the chair. "My God, I'd better toast you with an *espresso* or something."

"He doesn't think we ought to get into any recriminations, though," Spencer went on. "Frankly, I don't want that. And neither should you."

Annie leaned forward and stared at him. Spencer was on his old track again—pretending to himself and to her that they were something to each other that they were not. She laughed and leaned back again. "But that's wonderful *news,* Spencer. You really surprised me."

He glanced at her angrily. Her laugh faded. "Whatever you say won't make any difference," he said. "I'm in too deep now. I've got to go ahead. I can't go back."

"But, Spencer—" She reached across the table to touch his hand. He drew back quickly, pushing his chair a few inches away from the table.

"Dr. Blauberman could see immediately that Bobbie was very good for me," Spencer said. "I was slow at first, frankly. Dr. Blauberman recognized it before I did."

Annie smiled. She felt a rush of affection for Spencer.

"I'm sorry I didn't ask," she said. "Bobbie who? You got me so rattled."

219

"You don't know her," he said. "Dr. Blauberman warned me you'd probably be bitter."

"*What?*"

"You might feel bitter, after everything we had together, but you'll get over it," Spencer said.

Annie thought for a moment that he was joking, but then she saw an expression of rage on his face. He was perfectly serious. She began to feel bruised. "We had nothing together, Spencer, for crying out loud," she said. "What's the *matter* with you? We were together because Josh worked nights and Dr. Blauberman kept pushing you to come around—I was supposed to be good for your ego or something. I don't want to go into all that nonsense, Spencer, but for crying out loud—'everything we had together.' Who you kidding?" Annie found, unhappily, that she had raised her voice, and she sounded plaintive. Spencer noticed it, too. He didn't look quite so angry.

"I told Bobbie all about you," he said. "But it's better that you two don't meet."

"Well, sure, Spencer," Annie said.

"I didn't want Bobbie to think that I was doing this behind your back."

"But, Spencer, you weren't doing anything *behind* my back or in *front* of my back. You told me that it was good for business to be seen with a girl, with me, and I made myself available, and—" She stopped. He was pushing her into an argument, and the more she said, the more ridiculous it all sounded. "What are you arguing about?" she said, and heard her voice rising again. "You *know* the way it was."

Spencer gave a little smile. "You went around with me," he said.

"What have you told her?" Annie said, knowing she sounded desperate.

220

As usual, Spencer didn't seem to hear her. "I may be biting off more than I can chew, but Dr. Blauberman thinks Bobbie is a lovely individual," he said.

Annie tried to look impressed.

"She wants a lot of children," he said. "I've decided I want a lot of children, too. I'm giving her the ring tomorrow, but Dr. Blauberman said I had to have it out with you before I give her the ring."

"Have *what* out with me?"

"Frankly, I've changed," Spencer said.

"What's the *matter* with you, Spencer?" Annie felt a real sob coming on.

"Feelings change," Spencer went on in a rush. "This one probably won't last, either. Nothing lasts."

He was beginning to sound more familiar now. As she had done so often in the past, Annie felt called upon to reassure him.

"You know my old theory," she said, trying to make the uncomfortable tone in her voice go away. "If it lasts ten years, that's a lot—a lifetime."

"Frankly, I can't back out now even if I wanted to," Spencer said, and he looked angry again.

"You'll *love* being married, Spencer," she said. "Once you're in it, you're going to love all of it."

"Stockings hanging in the bathroom?" Spencer said.

"All of it," Annie said. "You'll enjoy it. Once you find yourself in it. You will. I know it." She sounded to herself like somebody giving a pep talk. But she believed it. It seemed important to make him see that she believed it.

"You always baffled me, frankly," he said. "My feeling about you changed, that's all. That's life."

"I'm very *happy* for you, Spencer," Annie said, feeling that she might cry.

"After all, we never had a physical relationship," Spencer said.

"There was nothing to have a physical relationship *about*," Annie said.

"These things end, that's all," he continued. "That's all we have to tell people."

"*What?*"

"Frankly, my mother was thrown when I told her," Spencer said.

"*I* never misled your mother about us," Annie said.

"I know it's tough, but I can't do anything to change things now," Spencer said. He rubbed his eye with his knuckle. She saw him looking at her with such melodramatic wariness that she felt the rush of affection once more.

"Spencer, you're such a dope," she said.

From wary, he started looking crafty. "Dr. Blauberman warned me that you'd try to make me feel guilty," he said. "People don't like it when you get well. They don't like it when you start to change. Dr. Blauberman always warned me about that."

"Oh, Lord," Annie said.

"I'm going ahead," Spencer said, angrily.

"Listen," Annie said. "Please, try to hear what I'm saying, Spencer. You have something solid now." She tried to smile. "What do you want of me? You don't have to pretend anything any more."

She tried again to recall the tune of "Kind Regards," but she found that the melody she had been carrying around in her head for days was gone. She felt alarm.

Seeing the expression of alarm on her face, Spencer seemed to relax. He no longer looked angry. He seemed satisfied. Evidently, Annie understood, he wanted her expression of alarm. Grief, shock, alarm—any of these reactions would have served the purpose. It was a sign he had come for. If he could make the moment of parting real, all the rest of it, back through the years, would be real, and he could move on; he would have something to play his life against.

"Be happy, Spencer," she said.

Spencer nodded, packed up his new-found past, and stood up to go. He rubbed his eye again. Then he was off and running.